I0647357

CONTENTS

Introduction .... Page   3

Ghost with a Gun .... Page   4

Night of Fear .... Page   70

Operation Silver Bullets .... Page   136

Night Witch .... Page   202

Cover Gallery .... Page   268

About Commando .... Page   279

The Commando Team

Editorial
Georgia Battle, Kate McAuliffe, Daniel McGachey,
Michelle O' Donnell, Gordon Tait

Design Editor
Leon Strachan

Designer
Grant Wood

Editor-in-chief
Alexandria Turner

Head of Children's Publishing
Gareth Whelan

Head of Magazines
Maria T. Welch

Published by DC Thomson & Co. Ltd.,
2 Albert Square, Dundee, DD1 1DD.

©DC Thomson & Co. Ltd. 2022

This volume collects material originally published in Commando issues
No. 104 in 1964, No. 984 in 1975, No. 5381 in 2020, and No. 5519 in 2022.

Some pages may contain references which are of their time but would not be considered
suitable today.

Email: generalenquiries@commandomag.com

www.commandocomics.com

Dear Readers,

Welcome, witchfinders and ghostbusters, to Commando's Fear Files Volume One, a collection of comics to thrill and shock you! Within the pages of this grim grimoire are four comics, each featuring an archetype of All Hallows' Eve from ghosts to werewolves and vampires to witches!

The first, #104 'Ghost with a Gun', is a tale from the 1960s where the soldiers didn't stay dead! In this yarn, ghosts hate the jerries as much as the yanks they fight with – and they're determined to take them back with them to the grave!

The second, #984 'Night of Fear', will curdle your blood! This 1975 Commando is set in the terrifying land of Transylvania, in the homeland of a certain vampire you might know – Dracula! With a deadly swarm of bats forcing our hero to crash land in the dead of night, you'll want to keep your garlic close at hand!

We move to modern Commandos with #5381 Operation Silver Bullets! Published in 2020, this comic is about a furry variety of German soldier – experimented on in a creepy castle! What big ears they have, what big eyes...and never mind their teeth!

Finally, #5519 Night Witch features the exploits of the famous soviet 588th Night Bomber regiment nicknamed Night Witches by the Germans. Only there's more to one of these women than it seems. Careful who you make deals with in the middle of the woods!

We hope you enjoy these classic stories and modern tales resurrected to delight you on a dark night... just keep turning the pages... and DON'T look behind you!

The Commando Team.

GHOST WITH A GUN

50 YEARS
1964-2014

Corporal Benny Walker's name will never go down in history — but he was the leader of the strangest fighting patrol the British Army had ever known.

It was some patrol, that one! Benny, six yanks and a couple of ghosts. Yes, the ghosts wore uniforms too — and didn't they get mucked into the Germans!

Commando
THE GOLD COLLECTION

www.commandocomics.com

4

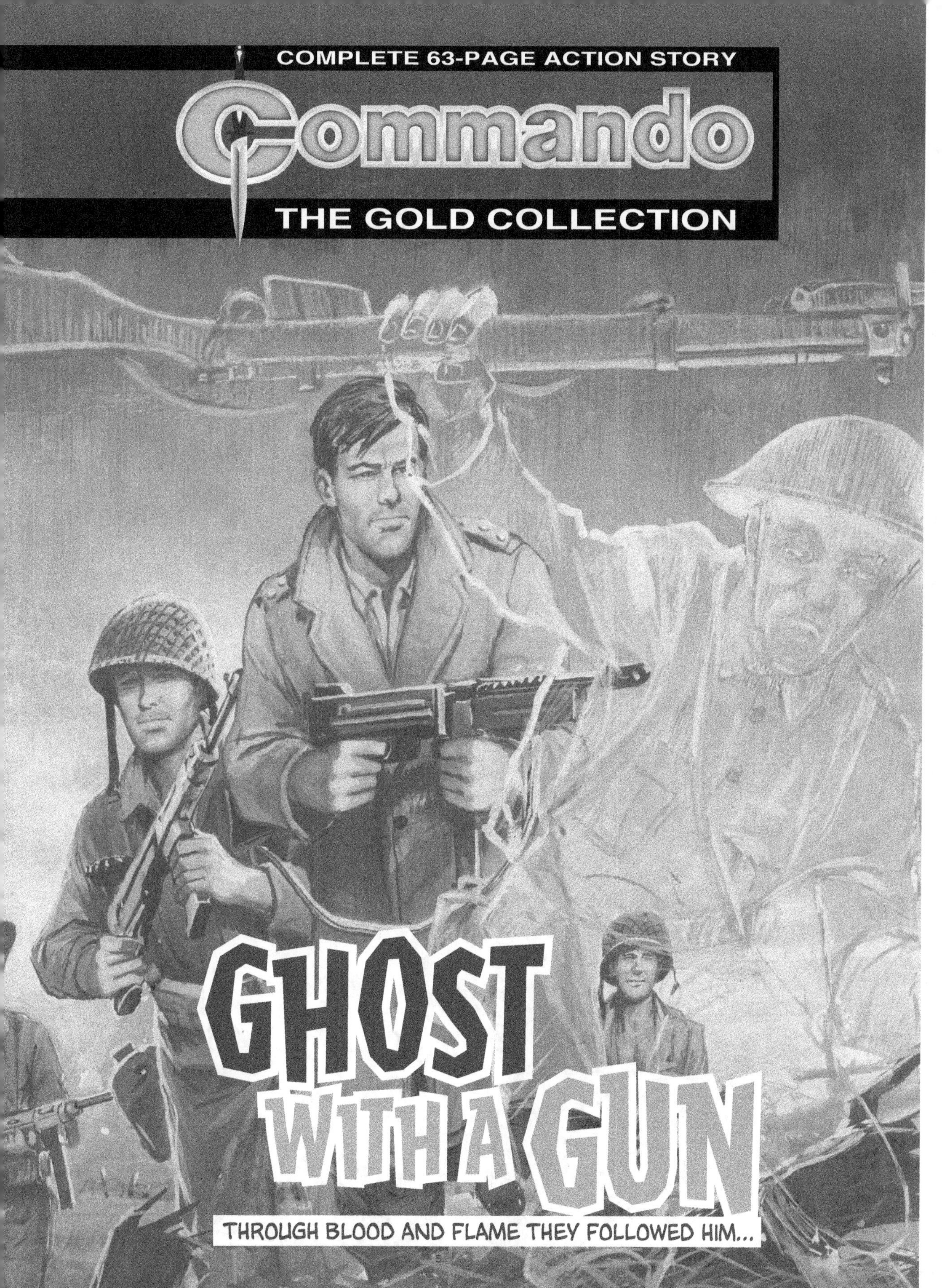
COMPLETE 63-PAGE ACTION STORY
Commando
THE GOLD COLLECTION
GHOST WITH A GUN
THROUGH BLOOD AND FLAME THEY FOLLOWED HIM...

Story: Du Feu

The writer credited as Du Feu is a person of mystery, so this won't be a very long biography. Du Feu's only contribution to *Commando* comics was #104 'Ghost with a Gun' and then they vanished. Rumoured to be a nom de plume by ex-editors, we're afraid we can't shed any more light on this creator.

Art: Francisco Cueto

Francisco Cueto i Marti was born in Barcelona in 1935. In the 1950s, he found work in the British Comics industry through the Bardon Art agency focussing on American-style comic art including *Captain Miracle, Annie Oakley, and Young Marvelman*. In the 1960s and 1970s, Cueto drew for several DC Thomson publications including *Commando, Hotspur, Warlord, Star Love Stories, Diana*, and *The Hornet,* alongside work for the UK's Fleetway, German, Danish and Spanish comics.

Cover: Chaco

Chaco's full name was Joaquin Chacopino Fabre and he was a regular cover artist for *Commando* in the 1960s and 1970s. Born in Barcelona in 1926, Chaco was a heavyweight in comics art and illustration, working extensively in the German comics industry. Chaco took up art over his military service and entered cartooning in the 1950s. Through agencies such as Studiortega and Bardon Art, he created artwork for comic companies in Britain, Sweden, Denmark, Belgium, Germany, France and Italy. Chaco lived in England for a while but missed his family and so returned to Spain. Unfortunately, Chaco rarely signed or was credited on his commissions, but it can be estimated he illustrated some 20,000 covers throughout his prolific career.

Ghost

WITH A GUN

HOW COULD A HUSSAR OF WELLINGTON'S 1815 ARMY, AND A PRIVATE, KILLED IN THE 1914-18 WAR, COME BACK TO HAUNT A BRITISH CORPORAL, ALONE AND WEAK WITH FEVER, IN A DERELICT BELGIAN FARMHOUSE IN 1944?

... R.E.M.E. CORPORAL BEN WALKER DIDN'T KNOW THE ANSWER TO THAT QUESTION. BUT AS THE TWO GHOSTLY FIGURES CAME TOWARDS HIM, A COLD HAND SEEMED TO CLUTCH AT HIS HEART ... AND FOR THE FIRST TIME IN HIS LIFE BEN KNEW THE REAL MEANING OF FEAR!

BUT THIS STORY REALLY BEGINS A FEW HOURS EARLIER. BEN HAD BEEN LYING IN THE BACK OF A MILITARY AMBULANCE, JOLTING ALONG A PITTED, SNOW-COVERED ROAD, SOMEWHERE SOUTH-WEST OF BRUSSELS. BESIDE HIM LAY A BADLY WOUNDED BRITISH INFANTRY CAPTAIN, TED DUNCAN —

HOW DO YOU FEEL, SIR? ANY EASIER?

EASY ENOUGH, BEN, BUT I'VE HAD IT! 'FRAID I'LL HAVE TO MISS OUT ON THAT PINT O' BEST BITTER YOU PROMISED ME WHEN YOU GOT BACK HOME.

TED DUNCAN, MORTALLY WOUNDED, COULD FEEL THE VERY LIFE OOZING OUT OF HIM. BUT BEN WALKER WOULDN'T HEAR OF IT.

DON'T SAY THAT, SIR. YOU WOULDN'T DO A MEAN THING LIKE LEAVING ME TO HAVE THAT PINT ON ME OWN? I MEAN, SOLITARY DRINKING CAN BE VERY BAD FOR YOU — THAT'S THE WAY TO END UP IN HOSPITAL...

KEEP OUT OF HOSPITAL, BENNY — AT ALL COST, EH? SORRY TO BE A BORE, SON, BUT — OH, HO, WHAT'S THIS? WE'RE STOPPING...

THE COLD, MONOTONOUS JOURNEY HAD BEEN HALTED BY A DISPATCH RIDER WITH FRESH ORDERS FOR MAJOR SLOPER, IN CHARGE OF THE CONVOY.

I'VE HAD A JOB FINDING YOU, SIR. EVERYTHING'S SHOT UP BACK THERE, AND THE JERRIES ARE POURING THROUGH. NOBODY SEEMS TO KNOW WHETHER THEY'RE COMING OR GOING.

I KNOW. WE'VE BEEN RE-ROUTED TWICE ALREADY — LOOKS LIKE THIS IS GOING TO BE THE THIRD TIME, EH?

HANDING MAJOR SLOPER THE ORDERS, THE DISPATCH RIDER KICKED HIS MACHINE INTO LIFE AND ROARED OFF.

HULLO, SO WE'RE RE-ROUTED AGAIN, AND INTO THE BATTLE AREA THIS TIME. WE'VE GOT TO HELP OUT THE YANKS — THEY'RE BEING CUT TO RIBBONS BY THE JERRY PANZERS ON THE SOUTH FLANK...AND EVERY AVAILABLE AMBULANCE IS BEING CALLED IN TO HELP GET THEIR CASUALTIES AWAY.

BUT WHAT ABOUT TRUCK FIVE, SIR? THERE'S A COUPLE OF CASUALTIES IN THERE WHO NEED URGENT MEDICAL ATTENTION. WE CAN'T JUST DRAG THE POOR BLIGHTERS ALONG WITH US.

BUT THE ORDERS WERE TO HEAD STRAIGHT FOR THE BATTLE AREA. TIME WAS TOO PRECIOUS TO BOTHER ABOUT TWO MEN WHO LOOKED LIKE DYING IN ANY CASE.

THEY'LL JUST HAVE TO COME ALONG, ROKER. THIS IS AN EMERGENCY, AND WE CAN'T SPARE AN AMBULANCE FOR ONLY TWO MEN. TURN RIGHT HERE, AND HEAD EAST ALONG THIS ROAD FOR FOUR OR FIVE MILES.

VERY GOOD, SIR.

THE RUMBLE OF GUNS GREW LOUDER AS THE AMBULANCE COLUMN NEARED THE BATTLE AREA.

DUNNO HOW THEY EXPECT US TO GET ANY REST WITH ALL THIS BANGING GOING ON. BLOOMING INCONSIDERATE, I CALL IT!

IT SOUNDS LIKE WE'RE RUNNING INTO REAL TROUBLE, BENNY...MUST BE SLAP IN THE MIDDLE OF IT, BY THE SOUND OF THOSE SHELLS...

THEN, SUDDENLY AMBULANCE 5, WITH THE TWO CASUALTIES ABOARD, RAN OUT OF LUCK. A NAZI SHELL EXPLODED ALMOST UNDER THE FRONT WHEELS.

THAT'S AS FAR AS WE'RE GOING, MATE. I'M OUT OF A JOB NOW — THIS OLD WAGON DON'T NEED A DRIVER ANYMORE. IT'LL NEED A CRANE TO MOVE IT ANYWHERE.

WE BETTER GET THEM TWO BLOKES IN THE BACK UNDER COVER. THAT OLD FARMHOUSE OVER THERE LOOKS LIKE IT MIGHT DO.

WHAT HAVE YOU STOPPED FOR THEN, MATE — TRAFFIC LIGHTS?
END OF THE LINE, ALL CHANGE! RECKON YOU CAN WALK IT A FEW YARDS TO THAT OLD FARM HOUSE WHILE WE CART IN THE CAPTAIN?
SHIVERING WITH FEVER, BENNY TURNED TO GRAB A BUNDLE OF BLANKETS FROM THE AMBULANCE. MEANWHILE THE AMBULANCE CREW WERE CARRYING THE DYING CAPTAIN TOWARDS THE ANCIENT STONE FARMHOUSE.
SAVE ME A ROOM THAT CATCHES THE MORNING SUN, BOYS!
PERHAPS THE GENTLEMAN WOULD LIKE TO RESERVE THE ROYAL SUITE?

BUT THEY WERE NEVER TO REACH THE FARMHOUSE — THERE WAS THE SHRILL WHINE OF A GERMAN SHELL, AND THE EAR-SPLITTING EXPLOSION THAT FOLLOWED BLASTED THEM ASIDE.

THEY'VE BOUGHT IT! THEY'VE BOUGHT IT! HEY, CAPTAIN DUNCAN — TED!

THE AMBULANCE MEN WERE KILLED OUTRIGHT BY THE BURSTING SHELL, AND CAPTAIN DUNCAN LAY CRUMPLED IN THE SNOW...

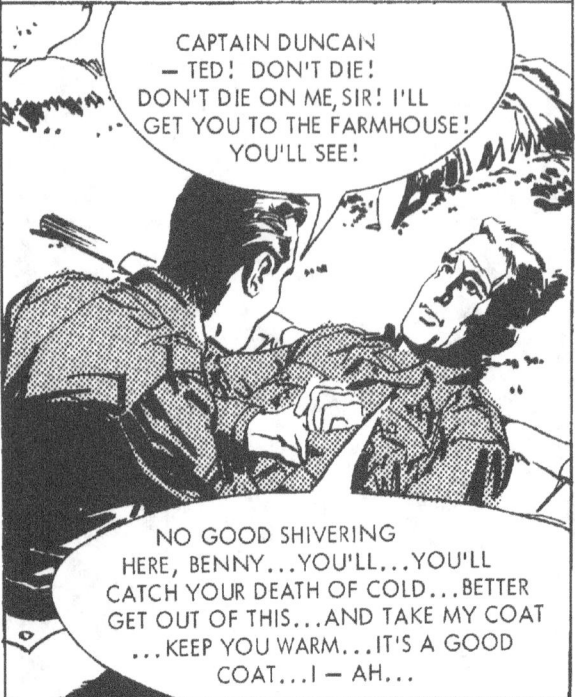

CAPTAIN DUNCAN — TED! DON'T DIE! DON'T DIE ON ME, SIR! I'LL GET YOU TO THE FARMHOUSE! YOU'LL SEE!

NO GOOD SHIVERING HERE, BENNY...YOU'LL...YOU'LL CATCH YOUR DEATH OF COLD...BETTER GET OUT OF THIS...AND TAKE MY COAT ...KEEP YOU WARM...IT'S A GOOD COAT...I — AH...

AND AS THE YOUNG OFFICER'S LIMP BODY FELL BACK, BENNY PICKED UP HIS COAT AND STAGGERED TO HIS FEET. THEN, BRACING HIS WASTED BODY AGAINST THE PANGS OF MALARIA, HE STUMBLED TOWARDS THE SHELTER OF THE FARMHOUSE, SICK, COLD AND ALONE.

I RECKON I WON'T BE LONG IN JOINING YOU, CAPTAIN. NOT MUCH CHANCE IN THIS FREEZING, LOUSY, HOLE.

SOMEHOW BENNY STRUGGLED TO THE SHELTER OF THE FARMHOUSE. THEN, ABSOLUTELY ALL-IN, HE CRUMPLED TO THE FLOOR.

F.B. 1815
T.T. 1917

MADE IT — JUST!
BY CRIKEY, IT'S COLD!
HOPE SOMEBODY COMES
ALONG SOON — JERRIES OR
ANYTHING, ELSE I'VE HAD IT.
...HALLO — WHAT'S THIS?
SOMEONE BEEN HERE BEFORE
ME — CARVING THE JOINT UP
WITH THEIR INITIALS TOO.

BUT THOUGH BENNY DIDN'T KNOW IT YET, THE OLD FARMHOUSE ROQUEBRUNE HAD SURVIVED OTHER WARS, AND SHELTERED OTHER SOLDIERS IN BY-GONE DAYS...

TROOPER FRED BOWLING AND RIFLEMAN TOMMY THOMPSON HAD STAYED, AND EACH IN TURN HAD LEFT A MEMENTO OF HIS STAY — THE INITIALS CARVED INTO THE OLD STONE WALL — THE INITIALS BENNY WALKER HAD SEEN JUST BEFORE HE COLLAPSED INTO AN EXHAUSTED, DELIRIOUS SLEEP.

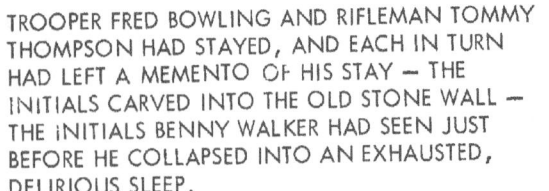

AND AS HE LAY COLD AND ALONE, DELIRIOUS WITH FEVER, BENNY WAS VISITED BY THE TWO SOLDIERS WHO HAD ONCE SHELTERED IN THE SAME OLD FARMHOUSE.

HULLO MATES — HOW DID YOU GET IN? ANYWAY, THERE'S PLENTY OF ROOM, AND I'LL BE GLAD OF THE COMPANY. MAKE YOURSELVES AT HOME.

THEN SUDDENLY BENNY SAT BOLT UPRIGHT. THOSE WERE NO MODERN SOLDIERS. THE UNIFORMS WERE YEARS OUT OF DATE.

NO! WAIT! THOSE UNIFORMS... YOU...YOU'RE DEAD MEN...GHOSTS. GET OUT OF HERE — GET OUT!

BENNY — LISTEN TO US, PLEASE...!

WE'RE MATES, BENNY — MATES!

BUT BENNY DIDN'T WANT MATES LIKE THESE. HIS LIPS WERE DRY, AND HIS KNEES WERE LIKE JELLY AS HE CRINGED BACK INTO THE CORNER.

F.B. 1815.
T.T. 1917.

DON'T TURN YOUR BACK ON US, BENNY, PLEASE!

LEAVE ME ALONE! I DON'T WANT TO SEE YOU! I GOT ENOUGH TROUBLES WITHOUT BEING HAUNTED BY...BY YOU BLOKES...

BUT THE TWO FIGURES PERSISTED. AND WHEN THEY APPEALED TO BENNY'S LOYALTY, HIS ASTONISHMENT OVERCAME HIS FEAR —

DON'T LET US DOWN, BENNY... WE'RE COMRADES-IN-ARMS. YOU WOULDN'T DO WRONG BY A COMRADE?

HEY, JUST A MINUTE, FANCYPANTS, NOT SO FAST. SINCE WHEN WERE YOU A COMRADE OF MINE? YOU WERE DEAD BEFORE I WAS EVEN BORN. NOW ALL I WANT IS FOR YOU TO STAY DEAD AND LEAVE ME ALONE!

...AND ALL THIS TALK ABOUT LETTING YOU DOWN IS SO MUCH HOG-WASH. WHAT COULD I DO FOR A GHOST?

THERE IS SOMETHING... THERE IS, BENNY! LISTEN...

AND TROOPER BOWLING OF THE 2ND ESHER HORSE BEGAN TO TELL HIS STORY...

IT WAS 1815, AND THERE WE WERE ALL WAITING FOR THE FRENCHIES. BONAPARTE WAS DOWN NEAR PARIS AND WE WERE UP AROUND BRUSSELS, US AND THE DUTCH AND THE PRUSSIANS... WAITING FOR HIM!

IN THESE MOMENTOUS DAYS BEFORE WATERLOO, WELLINGTON'S ARMY, SPREAD ALONG A 50-MILE FRONT AWAITED NAPOLEON'S ADVANCE. REGULAR DISPATCHES WENT TO THE OUTPOSTS ORDERING RECCES OF THE FRENCH POSITIONS...

YOU TWO, BOWLING AND MACDONNEL, ARE TO RIDE WITH CAPTAIN FOSTER DUE SOUTH TO TOIRE. RIGHT THEN, ME LADS, GET SADDLED UP.

VERY GOOD, SERGEANT.

HOW MANY MILES TO THIS PLACE, TOIRE, SIR?

ABOUT TWENTY MILES, TROOPER. WE'LL DO IT BY NIGHT -FALL, AND THEY'LL BE ABLE TO GET A RECONNAISSANCE PARTY OUT AND BACK BY MORNING.

IS IT IMPORTANT, SIR?

IN WAR EVERY ORDER IS IMPORTANT! YOU OUGHT TO KNOW THAT, BOWLING. BUT THIS IS ESPECIALLY SO! OUR GENERALS MUST GET MORE INFORMATION ABOUT BONEY'S MOVEMENTS!

WELL, IT SOUNDS SIMPLE ENOUGH, SIR — JUST RIDE TO TOIRE...

JUST RIDE TO TOIRE...BUT AS TORRENTIAL RAIN SWEPT DOWN AND A THICK MIST SWIRLED ACROSS THE DESOLATE COUNTRY ROADS, THE TASK GREW LESS AND LESS SIMPLE.

WHAT O'CLOCK IS IT SIR?

IT'S NINE O'CLOCK. WE WOULD HAVE BEEN AT TOIRE TWO HOURS AGO IF IT HADN'T BEEN FOR THIS DRATTED MIST AND RAIN!

AND THOUGH THEY DIDN'T KNOW IT, IN THE FALLING DUSK AND THE RAIN, THEY HAD MISSED THE ALLIED OUTPOSTS AND WERE NOW RIDING STRAIGHT TOWARDS THE FRENCH LINES.

LOOK SIR. FOUR HORSEMEN UP YONDER, LET'S HAIL THEM. THEY'LL BE ABLE TO DIRECT US.

LOOK AGAIN, TROOPER! LOOK AT THEIR HELMETS!

THE DISTANT HORSEMEN WEREN'T BRITISH AS BOWLING HAD THOUGHT AT FIRST.

THEY'RE FRENCHIES, AND THEY'VE SPOTTED US. COME ON, LET'S GET BACK!

RIGHT WITH YOU, SIR!

DESPERATELY THEY URGED THEIR WEARY HORSES BACK TOWARDS THE SAFETY OF THE BRITISH LINES, THEN SUDDENLY —

AH...SHE'S STUMBLED...

ARE YOU ALL RIGHT, SIR?

AND AS THE FRENCH CAVALRYMEN BORE DOWN UPON THE UNHORSED CAPTAIN, MACDONNEL AND BOWLING PULLED IN THEIR HORSES.

COME ON, BACK TO THE CAPTAIN!

WITH YOU, PADDY! WITH YOU!

THE FIGHT WAS BRIEF AND BITTER AS SABRE CLASHED WITH SABRE.

QUICK, BOWLING. GET INTO THEM, MAN!

DON'T LOOK LIKE WE'VE GOT MUCH OF A CHANCE HERE...

AND AS HE SAW MACDONNEL CUT DOWN BY THE FRENCH SABRES, BOWLING MADE A DECISION THAT WAS TO COST HIM DEAR...

THIS IS SHEER MURDER. I — I'VE GOT TO GET OUT OF HERE!

COME BACK! COME BACK AND GIVE ME A HAND, BLAST YOUR COWARDLY GUTS!

BUT BOWLING RODE ON, WITH THE DYING CAPTAIN'S WORDS RINGING IN HIS EARS.

A CURSE ON YOU TO ALL ETERNITY, YOU LILY-LIVERED DOG...

I'VE GOT TO GET AWAY...

BUT TROOPER FRED BOWLING DIDN'T GET FAR. A FRENCH RIFLEMAN'S BULLET CUT SHORT HIS FLIGHT.

SO, MORTALLY WOUNDED, I CREPT IN HERE TO DIE, A TREACHEROUS COWARD CONDEMNED TO WAIT HERE UNTIL —

CONDEMNED? WHAT ARE YOU TALKING ABOUT?

BUT BEFORE BENNY COULD FIND OUT MORE, TOMMY THOMPSON INTERRUPTED.

YES, CONDEMNED, LIKE ME. LISTEN TO MY STORY THEN YOU'LL KNOW.

AND TOMMY THOMPSON, CONDEMNED LIKE FRED BOWLING TO FIND NO REST, EVEN IN DEATH, TOLD HIS STORY.

IT WAS JUNE 1917. IT HAD BEEN A LONG, LOUSY WAR. AND I WAS SICK TO THE TEETH OF IT. I WAS IN THE HUNDRED-AND-TWELFTH REGIMENT OF FOOT.

AFTER THE GERMAN LINE HAD BEEN POUNDED FOR HOURS BY A
MURDEROUS ARTILLERY BARRAGE, TOMMY AND THE REST OF B
COMPANY HAD GONE OVER THE TOP WITH THE FIRST WAVE.

DON'T THEM
JERRIES EVER GIVE
UP? THAT LAST BARRAGE
SHOULD HAVE KNOCKED
ALL THE FIGHT OUT OF
'EM!

THE GERMANS SAVAGELY DROVE BACK THE FIRST BRITISH ATTACK,
AND THE SURVIVORS OF B COMPANY BEAT A HASTY RETREAT.
BUT THERE WAS NO RETREAT FOR TOMMY THOMPSON, WHO LAY
UNCONSCIOUS AT THE BOTTOM OF A GERMAN TRENCH.

CHASE THE
SCHWEINHUND
ENGLANDERS BACK
TO THEIR PIG-
STIES!

GET THESE PRISONERS OUT OF THE WAY BEFORE THE BRITISHERS COME AGAIN. HURRY!

RAUS! QUICK, ENGLANDER. ON YOUR FEET!

TOMMY, ALONG WITH OTHER P.O.W.'S, SOON FOUND HIMSELF BEING HERDED ON TO A TRAIN BOUND FOR GERMANY — AND CAPTIVITY ...

SO THAT'S THE WAY IT ENDS! WELL, I CAN'T SAY I'M SORRY. THREE LOUSY YEARS IN THE TRENCHES IS ENOUGH FOR ANY MAN, I RECKON!

BUT THE WAR WASN'T OVER YET FOR TOMMY. ON THE TRAIN, AN ESCAPE PLAN WAS HATCHED, AND HE WAS BROUGHT IN ON IT.

NOW WE ALL KNOW WHAT TO DO. SO WHEN I GIVE THE SIGNAL, WE MOVE...

I RECKON IT'S MAD. STILL, ONE FOR ALL AND ALL FOR ONE, AND ALL THAT JOLLY OLD STUFF, I SUPPOSE...

THE PLAN WAS TO RUSH THE NEAREST GUARDS AND THEN UNCOUPLE THE TRUCK BEFORE THE GUARDS IN THE REST OF THE TRAIN COULD BE ALERTED...

COME ON, MATE, WE'VE NEARLY DONE IT.

BUT BEFORE THEY COULD GIVE THE FINAL HEAVE THAT WOULD UNCOUPLE THE TRUCK, A GERMAN GUARD SUDDENLY APPEARED FROM ABOVE AND SMASHED TOMMY'S MATE DOWN AMONG THE CHURNING WHEELS. TOMMY CAME JUST TOO LATE TO SAVE HIM, BUT —

BUT AS THE GERMAN SLITHERED, SCREAMING, UNDER THE WHEELS, TOMMY THOMPSON'S STRENGTH SEEMED TO DESERT HIM. PARALYSED WITH FEAR, HE COULDN'T MOVE TO FREE THE COUPLING.

AND WITH A RECKLESS LEAP TOMMY LAUNCHED HIMSELF OFF THE BUCKING RAIL TRUCK.

THE LITTLE SWINE'S GONE AND JUMPED OUT ON US...

YOU GUTLESS RAT! YOU'LL SUFFER FOR WHAT YOU'VE DONE!

LOOK OUT! HERE COME THE REST OF THE GUARDS!

AND, WITH HIS MIND A WHIRLPOOL OF CONFLICTING THOUGHTS, TOMMY HAD SET OFF BLINDLY TO MAKE HIS WAY BACK TOWARDS HIS OWN LINES. BUT BY A CRUEL TWIST OF FATE HE STUMBLED STRAIGHT INTO THE BRITISH SHELL-BARRAGE, AND FINALLY, EXHAUSTED, AND MORTALLY WOUNDED BY SHRAPNEL, HE CRAWLED INTO THE ROQUEBRUNE FARM TO DIE.

TO DIE, BUT NEVER TO REST. THERE NEVER WILL BE ANY REST FOR ME AND FRED HERE, UNLESS...UNLESS...

WELL, OUT WITH IT! UNLESS WHAT?

NO! FIRST YOU MUST JUDGE. WE LET OUR COMRADES DOWN. YOU'VE HEARD OUR STORIES, AND NOW YOU MUST DECIDE IF YOU WANT TO HELP US.

WELL, JUDGING ISN'T EXACTLY MY SPECIALITY. YOU'VE DONE WRONG, VERY WRONG — NO DOUBT OF THAT. YOU WERE COWARDS, AND YOU'VE SUFFERED FOR IT, TOO. BUT IT DON'T SEEM RIGHT A MAN SHOULD GO ON AND ON SUFFERING FOR ONE WRONG ACT. NOT IN MY BOOK, LEASTWAYS!

THEN, YOU WILL HELP US?

IN HIS WEAKENED STATE BENNY WAS BEGINNING TO ACCEPT THE TWO GHOSTS, TALKING TO THEM AS IF THEY WERE REAL.

HOLD YOUR HORSES! WHEN IT COMES TO HELPING, THAT'S A DIFFERENT KETTLE O' FISH. I'D LIKE TO, IF I COULD, BUT...

BUT YOU CAN! IF WE COULD MAKE UP FOR OUR COWARDICE BY DOING GOOD.

IF! BUT WE CAN'T! ONLY THE LIVING CAN — AND YOU COULD DO GOOD FOR US...BE BRAVE FOR US, BENNY. WE'LL HELP AS MUCH AS WE CAN — AND THEN THAT WAY WE CAN WIPE THE SLATE CLEAN.

28

BUT BENNY SHOOK HIS HEAD. IT JUST WASN'T POSSIBLE.

LOOK MATES, I'D LIKE TO HELP YOU OUT, BUT BE REALISTIC. I'M HERE ON ME OWN AND I'M NEARLY PEGGING OUT WITH MALARIA. I HAVEN'T EVEN GOT A GUN, AND IF I HAD — WELL, FIGHTING'S NOT MY JOB. I'M A MECHANIC, NOT A BLOOMING COMMANDO!

BENNY KNEW HIS OWN CAPABILITIES, AND THERE WAS JUST NOTHING HE COULD DO. THE ODDS AGAINST HIM WERE FAR TOO GREAT ...

I MEAN IF THERE WAS SOME-ONE TO...HALLO, LOOK WHO'S HERE! GOOD TO SEE YOU CAPTAIN DUNCAN, SIR; IT'S ME, BENNY...

BENNY WAS DELIGHTED TO SEE A FACE HE KNEW. IT WAS TED DUNCAN, THE YOUNG OFFICER WHO'D BEEN HIS COMPANION IN THE AMBULANCE.

BOY, AM I GLAD TO SEE YOU! LISTEN, SIR, STRAIGHTEN THESE TWO OUT, WILL YOU? THEY WANT ME TO — I DON'T KNOW — WIN A V.C. OR SOMETHING. TELL THEM IT'S IMPOSSIBLE, SIR. YOU UNDERSTAND...

NO, BENNY. THERE'S WORK FOR YOU TO DO, AND YOU CAN DO IT. TRUST ME, BENNY. I'LL HELP YOU...WE'LL ALL HELP YOU, BUT YOU MUST TRUST US AND TRY. THERE IS IMPORTANT WORK FOR YOU TO DO.

WHILE BENNY LISTENED IN STUNNED SILENCE TO THE GHOSTLY VOICE OF CAPTAIN DUNCAN, GERMAN PANZERS WERE SWEEPING FORWARD WITH THE NAZI COUNTER-ATTACK. BRITISH H.Q., AWAY TO THE SOUTH, ANXIOUSLY WAITED FOR DETAILED INFORMATION ABOUT THE STRENGTH OF THAT ATTACK.

THEY'LL BE THROUGH TO US ON THE RADIO AS SOON AS THEY'VE GOT THE FACTS, SIR.

NOTHING THROUGH YET? LET US KNOW IMMEDIATELY THERE IS. THANK YOU, SERGEANT.

IT WAS JUST A CASE OF WAITING FOR DEFINITE INFORMATION ABOUT THE STRENGTH OF THE GERMAN COUNTER-ATTACK.

NOTHING WE CAN DO! AIR RECONNAISSANCE IS OUT OF THE QUESTION WITH THESE CLOUD CONDITIONS, AND OUR GROUND INTELLIGENCE CAN'T HELP. IT'S UP TO THE FRENCH RESISTANCE JOHNNIES TO FIND OUT FOR US.

LET'S HOPE THEY'RE QUICK. THE OLD MAN'S SENT DOWN ANOTHER VERY URGENT MEMO SCREAMING FOR INFORMATION. HE'S GOT TO KNOW...

...BECAUSE IF JERRY'S REALLY PUTTING HIS WEIGHT INTO THIS COUNTER-ATTACK, WE'LL HAVE TO MOVE UP HERE TO STRENGTHEN THE LINE BETWEEN BRUSSELS AND THE MEUSE...BUT FIRST WE'VE GOT TO KNOW WHAT'S HAPPENING!
BRUSSELS
RIVER
MEUSE
GERMAN FORCES

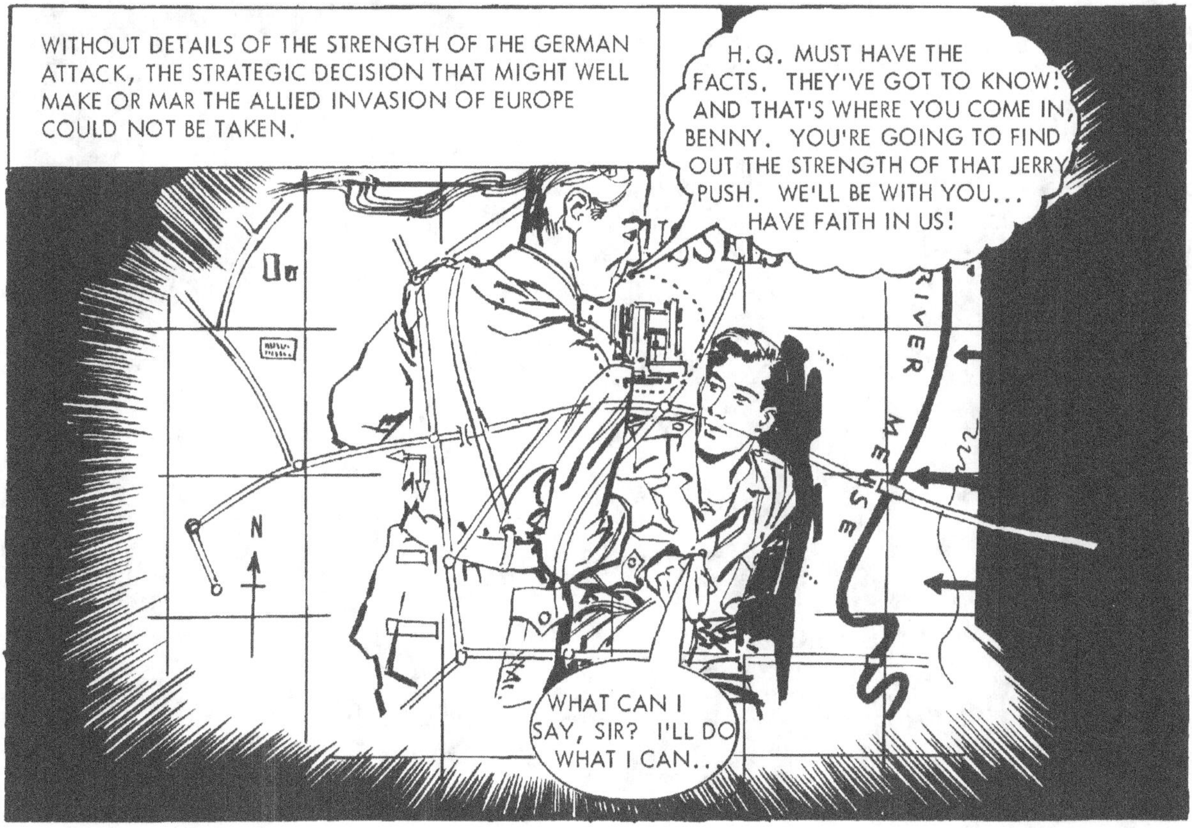
WITHOUT DETAILS OF THE STRENGTH OF THE GERMAN ATTACK, THE STRATEGIC DECISION THAT MIGHT WELL MAKE OR MAR THE ALLIED INVASION OF EUROPE COULD NOT BE TAKEN.
H.Q. MUST HAVE THE FACTS. THEY'VE GOT TO KNOW! AND THAT'S WHERE YOU COME IN, BENNY. YOU'RE GOING TO FIND OUT THE STRENGTH OF THAT JERRY PUSH. WE'LL BE WITH YOU... HAVE FAITH IN US!
RIVER
MEUSE
N
WHAT CAN I SAY, SIR? I'LL DO WHAT I CAN...

WE DONE WRONG, BUT DON'T TURN YOUR BACK ON US. WE'LL BE WITH YOU!

I'LL DO MY BEST FOR YOU, MATES.

AND THE WAY YOU HANDLE THIS JOB COULD MAKE UP FOR US, BENNY. REMEMBER THAT!

SILENTLY THE GHOSTS VANISHED, AND WITH THEM BENNY'S FEVER SEEMED TO VANISH TOO. BUT OUTSIDE THE FARM-HOUSE ALL WAS NOISE, AS THE NAZI PANZERS CRASHED THROUGH THE AMERICAN LINES.

AND A PARTY OF AMERICAN STRAGGLERS, HOPELESSLY LOST IN THE CONFUSION OF THE GERMAN ATTACK, EVENTUALLY FOUND THEMSELVES OUTSIDE THE FARMHOUSE ROQUEBRUNE.

WELL, WHAT DO YOU SAY? RECKON THIS IS AS GOOD A PLACE TO STOP AS ANY. IT AIN'T AS IF WE'RE GOING ANYWHERE!

THE AMERICANS WERE ALL TRUCK DRIVERS, NOT FIGHTING TROOPS...ONLY ONE OF THEM EVEN CARRIED A GUN. THE SIGHT OF BENNY FAST ASLEEP ON THE FLOOR BROUGHT THEM ALL UP SHORT —

WELL, WHAT DO YOU KNOW! ANY OF YOU GUYS OBJECT TO LIVING IN THE SAME HOTEL AS A LIMEY? PRETTY COOL CUSS BY THE LOOK OF HIM. SLEEPING IT OUT — HOW'S THAT FOR NERVE!

THAT'S WHAT I LIKE ABOUT THEM LIMEYS. IT CAN'T BE HIS TURN TO BAT YET, OR SOMETHING!

THE NOISE THE AMERICANS MADE GATHERING STICKS TO
LIGHT A FIRE SOON ROUSED BENNY FROM HIS SLEEP.
AND THE VOICE OF TOMMY THOMPSON WHISPERED IN
HIS EAR.

COME ON, MATE, THIS ISN'T A SAFE BILLET NO MORE — GET 'EM OUT OF HERE!

STRIKE ME PINK! WHAT'S THE STAR-SPANGLED BRIGADE DOING HERE? BREWING UP — EH? COME ON — THERE'S NO TIME TO HANG AROUND. WE GOTTA GET OUT OF HERE, QUICK!

GET OUT? WHAT ARE YOU TALKING ABOUT? WE JUST GOT HERE...SIR!

BENNY, SURPRISED AT BEING CALLED SIR,
SUDDENLY REMEMBERED CAPTAIN DUNCAN'S
GREAT-COAT.

THEY THINK THIS IS MY COAT, BUT THERE'S NO TIME FOR EXPLANATIONS NOW. I'VE GOT TO GET THEM OUT OF HERE. TOMMY SAID THE FARMHOUSE WASN'T SAFE.

BUT, SIR, WE'RE ALL THROUGH RUNNING! WE'VE BEEN BACK-PEDALLING SINCE FIRST LIGHT YESTERDAY. HERE WE ARE, AND I RECKON HERE IS WHERE WE SHOULD STAY.

BUT BENNY'S FEVER HAD PASSED, AND HIS STRENGTH HAD NOW RETURNED. SOMEHOW HE WAS ABSOLUTELY CERTAIN OF THE WAY AHEAD. HE KNEW WHAT HAD TO BE DONE.

AND THOUGH THEY WEREN'T TOO KEEN ON THE IDEA, THE AMERICANS FOLLOWED BENNY OUT OF THE HOUSE. HIS CERTAINTY AND INSISTENCE KEPT THEM MOVING.

LISTEN, YANK, YOU DO LIKE I SAY, OR YOU WON'T EVER RUN ANYWHERE AGAIN! WE'RE GETTING OUT OF HERE, OR ONCE THE BIG STUFF HITS US WE'LL ALL BE BLOWN TO SMITHEREENS.

OK, SIR — IF YOU SAY SO. BUT WHERE WE GOING TO? IT TOOK US ALL DAY TO FIND THIS PLACE.

LIKE I SAID, SIR, WHERE TO?

DON'T WORRY, CHUM. I KNOW WHERE WE'RE GOING. THE OLD FARMHOUSE IS GOING TO BE CLOBBERED ANY MINUTE NOW, YOU MARK MY WORDS.

AND JUST AS BENNY HAD PREDICTED, THERE WAS A SUDDEN NERVE-SHATTERING EXPLOSION FROM BEHIND THEM, AND THE OLD FARMHOUSE ROQUEBRUNE COLLAPSED IN A LAND-SLIDE OF DUST AND RUBBLE. A GERMAN 88MM. SHELL HAD SCORED A DIRECT HIT.

HOLY MACKEREL! BUT — BUT HOW DID YOU KNOW, SIR? BOY, WE SURE WERE LUCKY TO GET OUT OF THERE WHEN YOU SAID!

NOT LUCK ...NOT JUST LUCK...

BUT THE PATH THEY WERE FOLLOWING LED BACK TO THE VILLAGE OF ST. CLAIR...AND TROUBLE!

HEY, WHERE WE GOING? THIS IS THE WAY BACK TO THAT VILLAGE WE'VE JUST COME FROM. IT'S CHOCK FULL OF PANZERS!

I DUNNO. THE LIMEY OFFICER SAYS TO GET OUT OF THE FARM-HOUSE — AND HE'S DEAD RIGHT. NOW HE SAYS TO COME ON DOWN THIS PATH, SO MAYBE HE'S RIGHT AGAIN. ANYWAYS, YOU GOT A BETTER IDEA?

AND SO THEY FOLLOWED BENNY BACK TO THE VILLAGE THEY HAD JUST LEFT. HE WAS LEADING MEN FOR THE FIRST TIME IN HIS LIFE, AND IN SOME STRANGE WAY HE KNEW THAT EVERY ORDER HE GAVE WAS DEAD RIGHT.

HEY, SIR, WHERE DO YOU RECKON ON GOING? THIS ST. CLAIR JOINT IS FULL OF KRAUTS!

JUST KEEP GOING! ONCE WE MAKE THAT NEAREST HOUSE WE'LL BE OK.

BUT SUDDENLY A GERMAN ARMOURED PATROL THUNDERED INTO SIGHT ...

WHAT DID I SAY! THE PLACE IS MOVING WITH 'EM!

BUTTON YOUR LIP, BUSTER! NOBODY'S SHOT OUR EARS OFF YET. LET'S RIDE OUR LUCK A LITTLE. THE GUY SAYS ONCE WE REACH THAT HOUSE EVERYTHING'LL BE FINE. I GO ALONG WITH THAT!

KEEPING TO THE COVER OF THE BACKGROUND, BENNY LED THEM AT A CRAWL TOWARDS THE LITTLE FRENCH HOUSE.

THAT'S IT, BENNY — LIE DOGGO. THAT'S THE GAME!

THEY'VE SPOTTED US! C'MON LET'S RUN FOR IT!

KEEP DOWN! THEY HAVEN'T SEEN ANYTHING. THEY'RE JUST FIRING OFF — TESTING THEIR GUNS OR SOMETHING. WE'LL BE OK — I KNOW!

AND AS BENNY HAD PREDICTED, THEY REACHED THE HOUSE, UNDETECTED — AND FOUND AN UNEXPECTED WELCOME.

VENEZ, MES ENFANTS! QUICKLY, IN OUT OF THE COLD...AND THE BULLETS!

THE LIMEY WAS RIGHT AGAIN! FROM HERE ON I'M BACKING YOU ALL THE WAY, PAL!

UNERRINGLY BENNY HAD LED HIS LITTLE GROUP TO THE TEMPORARY SAFETY OF THE FRENCH RESISTANCE H.Q. — TO THE PLACE WHERE HE WAS NEEDED...

WE SAW YOU COMING, MON CAPITAINE. HEAVEN ALONE KNOWS HOW THE BOCHES DID NOT SEE YOU, TOO...BUT, VOILA, YOU ARE HERE, AND WELCOME. WE NEED YOUR HELP...

YES, I KNOW. THERE'S WORK TO BE DONE.

WORK? WHAT'S THIS? WHAT'S THE GUY GONNA DO NOW?

AND PIERRE QUICKLY EXPLAINED WHAT HAD TO BE DONE.

THIS COUNTER-ATTACK IS HITLER'S LAST GAMBLE. HE IS THROWING IN EVERY TANK AND EVERY SOLDIER HE CAN SPARE. HE HAS NO RESERVES AT ALL — THE SITUATION IS CRITICAL.

BUT DOES H.Q. KNOW EXACTLY HOW STRONG THE ATTACK IS? ARE THEY PREPARED FOR THIS BIG AN ONSLAUGHT?

THAT IS JUST IT! MY TASK WAS TO GET THE INFORMATION THROUGH TO ALLIED H.Q. BY RADIO. BUT WE HAD A LITTLE TROUBLE FROM THE BOCHES — I WAS THE ONLY ONE WHO ESCAPED, AND THE RADIO WAS DESTROYED. I WAS WOUNDED...

CAN'T YOU GET ANOTHER RADIO?

IF THERE IS ANOTHER RADIO, WE CAN GET TO IT ...AND TRANSMIT THE INFORMATION!

PIERRE SPREAD A MAP OUT ON THE TABLE, AND SHOWED THEM A VILLAGE WHERE THERE WAS ANOTHER SECRET RADIO TRANSMITTER.

SAY, BUT THAT'S ALL OF 20 MILES AWAY FROM HERE — AND THROUGH COUNTRY THAT'S MOVING WITH KRAUTS. WE WOULDN'T GET MORE THAN A MILE BEFORE THEY GAVE US THE CHOP!

WE'LL MAKE IT!

CAPTAIN DUNCAN AND TOMMY AND FRED WILL SEE WE DO!

I NEED NOT TELL YOU THAT THIS INFORMATION IS VITAL. YOU MUST SUCCEED. MY TWO MEN WOULD HELP, BUT THEY ARE TOO WELL KNOWN. BESIDES THEY HAVE NO GUNS!

BUT THE OTHER AMERICANS STILL HAD DOUBTS. THE VILLAGE OF LENGRES WAS TWENTY MILES AWAY ACROSS GERMAN-HELD TERRITORY.

DON'T LET HIM TALK US INTO IT, DAN. IT'S SUICIDE!

QUIT SQUAWKING, BUSTER! THIS GUY'S ALREADY SAVED OUR LIVES TWICE. WE DO LIKE HE SAYS — OK?

THERE WAS A CERTAIN GLINT IN DAN'S EYE THAT TOLD THE OTHER AMERICANS IT WAS USELESS TO ARGUE, AND SOON THEY WERE READY TO SET OFF AGAIN.

LET'S DRINK TO — TO OLD COMRADES...

WELL, MES BRAVES — GOOD LUCK!

AND AS THEY DRANK THE TOAST, BENNY KNEW THAT WHATEVER HAPPENED, HIS PARTICULAR OLD COMRADES WOULDN'T LET THEM DOWN...

LIKE TROOPER FRED BOWLING MANY YEARS BEFORE, BENNY HAD TO DELIVER A VITAL MESSAGE AND BOWLING'S HOPES WENT WITH HIM.

GOD SPEED, BENNY. IF I CAN HELP YOU TO SUCCEED WHERE I FAILED, I'LL HAVE MADE UP FOR THINGS, AND MY SPIRIT WILL REST AT LONG LAST.

ONLY BUSTER WAS STILL DOUBTFUL ABOUT THEIR CHANCES —

LISTEN, DAN, I'M A DRIVER — A NON-COM! SO ARE YOU, AND SO ARE THE REST OF US. WE'VE GOT ONE GUN BETWEEN US AND A COUPLE OF DOZEN ROUNDS OF AMMO. THE WHOLE DEAL'S SO CRAZY I GO PIE-EYED JUST THINKING ABOUT IT!

BUT DAN HAD TAKEN A BELLYFUL FROM THE COMPLAINING
BUSTER. OR MAYBE IT WAS JUST THAT HE COULDN'T JUSTIFY
HIS OWN BLIND CONFIDENCE IN THE LITTLE LIMEY.

SO HELP ME, BUSTER,
IF YOU DON'T BUTTON UP
THAT GRIPING LIP OF YOURS, I'LL
FILL YOU SO FULL OF HOLES YOU'LL
LOOK LIKE A WALKING HONEY-
COMB. WE DO LIKE THE LIMEY
SAYS — NOW MOVE!

BUT EVEN DAN COULDN'T COMPLETELY SUPPRESS THE
NIGGLING DOUBTS IN HIS MIND. THE LIMEY HAD BEEN
RIGHT SO FAR, BUT —

LOOK, SIR...ER...
DON'T YOU RECKON WE'RE
JUST A LITTLE SHORT ON WEAPONS
— I MEAN FOR AN ARMED PATROL
ONE GUN BETWEEN US AIN'T
EXACTLY A LOT!

YOU'LL HAVE TO
CAPTURE SOME ENEMY
MUSKETS, BENJAMIN.
IT'S THE ONLY WAY.

YOU'RE RIGHT
THERE, MATE.
MUSKETS — THAT'S
WHAT WE
NEED.

BENNY'S SUDDEN SLIP INTO THE LANGUAGE OF NAPOLEONIC TIMES WHEN HE MENTIONED MUSKETS, COMPLETELY BAFFLED DAN. BUT HE DIDN'T HAVE TIME TO PONDER IT, FOR SUDDENLY A COLUMN OF GERMAN INFANTRY APPEARED UP AHEAD.

GEE! THEM LIMEY'S SURE DO USE SOME MIGHTY STRANGE WORDS! MUSKETS — SOUNDS LIKE WE'RE STILL FIGHTING AT THE ALAMO OR SOMETHING...

HEY...OOP! LOOK OUT, SIR — KRAUTS UP AHEAD, COMING THIS WAY!

THEY DIVED INTO THE DEEP DITCH THAT RAN ALONG THE ROAD-SIDE.

OK, DAN, WE WANT WEAPONS, AND THEY'VE GOT WEAPONS. SO LET'S DO A DEAL — AT GUN-POINT. GIVE ME THE TOMMY AND LISTEN.

BENNY CRAWLED AWAY ALONG THE BOTTOM OF
THE DITCH. THEN, JUST WHEN THE NAZIS WERE
OPPOSITE THE SPOT WHERE THE AMERICANS WERE
CONCEALED, HE LEAPT OUT INTO THE MIDDLE
OF THE ROAD —

OK — LET'S
SEE YOU JUMP,
JERRIES.

WITH FAULTLESS FIELD-DISCIPLINE THE GERMANS ZIG-ZAGGED
FOR THE NEAREST COVER — WHICH HAPPENED TO BE THE ROAD-
SIDE DITCH. THEY DIVED IN — RIGHT INTO THE WAITING ARMS
OF THE AMERICANS!

YOU WON'T
BE NEEDING THE
GUN WHERE YOU'RE
GOING, KRAUT.

COME TO
PAPA, JERRY-
BOY!

THE GERMANS NEVER KNEW WHAT HIT THEM. STRONG HANDS WRESTED THEIR SCHMEISSERS FROM THEM. THERE WAS A FIERCE STACCATO CHATTER OF BULLETS...AND IT WAS ALL OVER.

HAPPY NOW, BUSTER? YOU'VE GOT YOURSELF A GUN ANYWAY.

SURE THING, SIR — AND BOY, IT FEELS MIGHTY GOOD!

THE SUCCESS OF THE AMBUSH SENT THE MORALE OF THE G.I.'S SOARING SKY-HIGH. ARMED AND CONFIDENT, THEY PRESSED ON — READY FOR ANYTHING.

I GOTTA HAND IT TO THE LIMEY, DAN. HE KNOWS WHAT HE'S DOING!

LIKE I SAID, BUSTER — THIS IS THE GUY TO FOLLOW IF WE WANNA GET BACK STATE-SIDE, ALL IN ONE PIECE!

BUT THE VILLAGE THEY HAD TO REACH WAS STILL A LONG WAY OFF...A LONG WAY TO WALK!

PITY WE COULDN'T HITCH A LIFT, BUSTER. FOUR WHEELS IS A MIGHT LESS TIRING THAN TWO LEGS.

YOU CAN SAY THAT AGAIN, PAL.

UP THERE'S THE PLACE FOR A ROAD BLOCK, BENNY.

AND ACTING ON TOMMY'S ADVICE, BENNY QUICKLY ORDERED THEM TO THE VANTAGE POINT WHICH THE FIRST WORLD WAR VETERAN HAD POINTED OUT.

COME ON, UP THERE BEYOND THE BEND. WE'LL BLOCK 'EM AS THEY COME ROUND THE CORNER. WE'LL HAVE TO RUN FOR IT, THOUGH.

WE'RE WITH YOU, CAPTAIN.

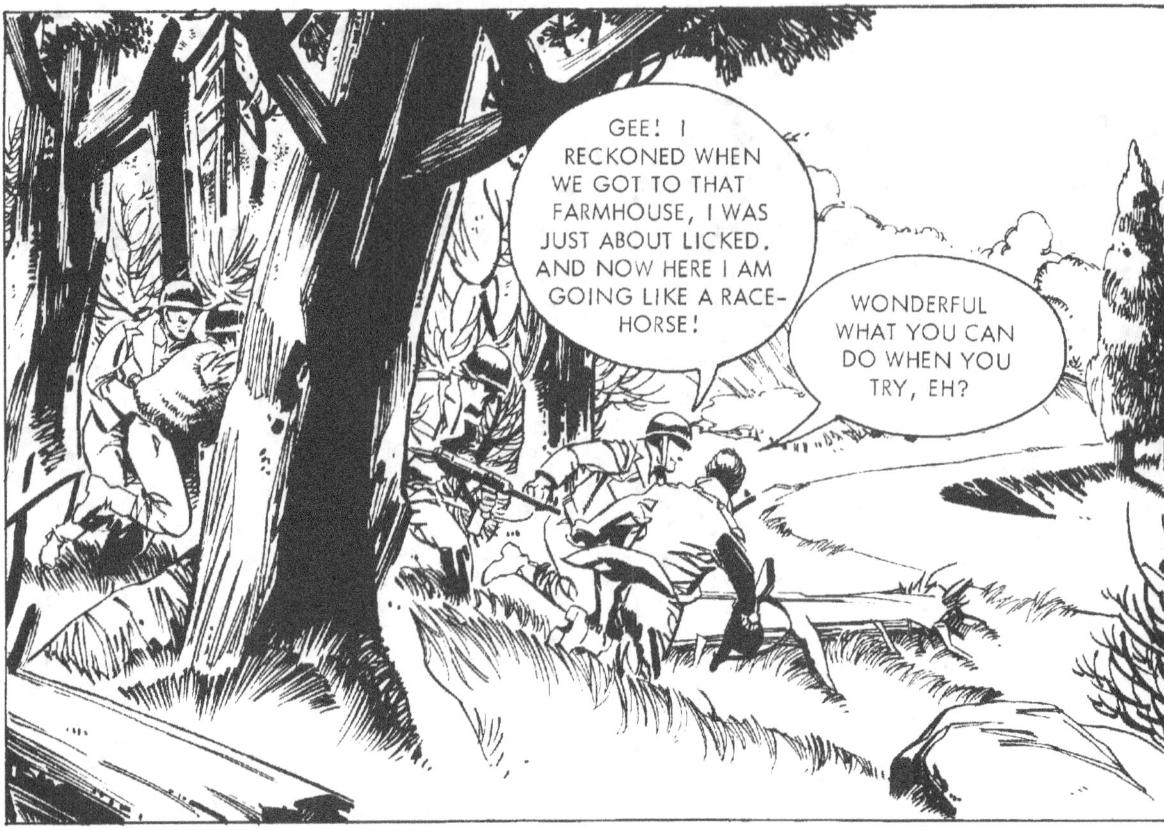

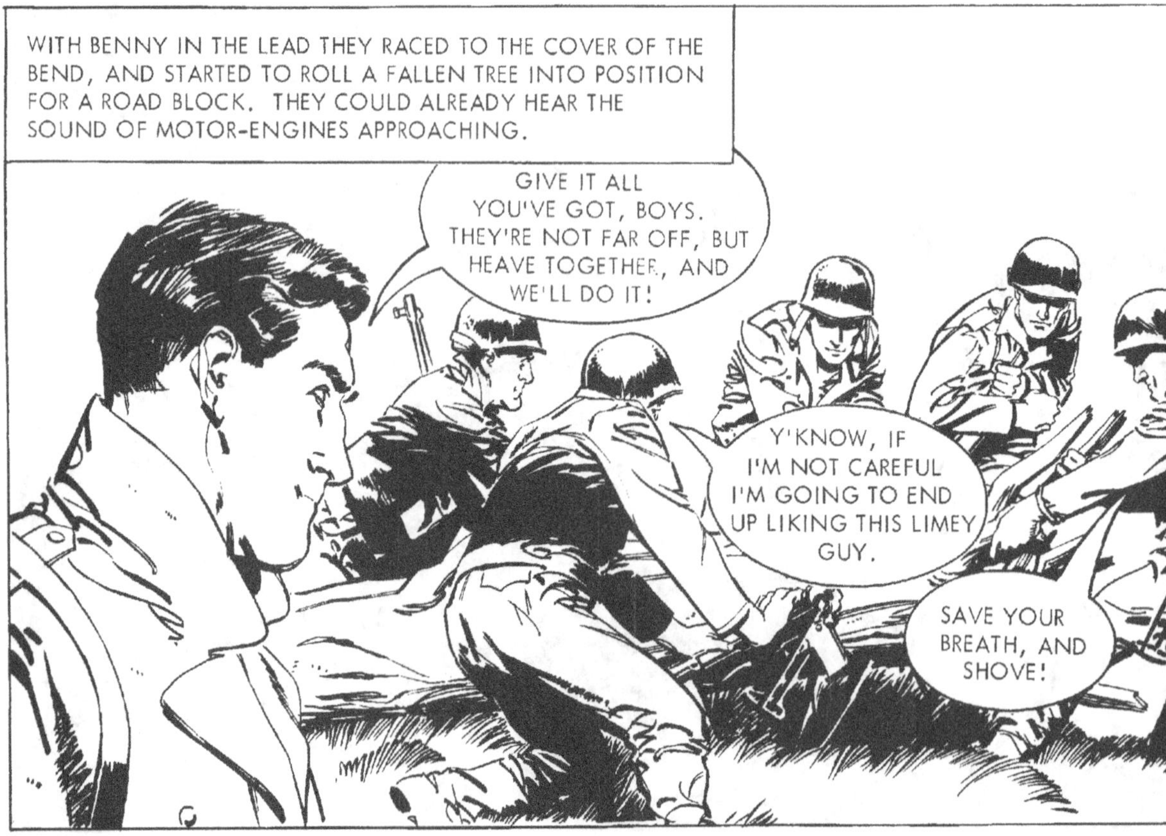

WITH BENNY IN THE LEAD THEY RACED TO THE COVER OF THE BEND, AND STARTED TO ROLL A FALLEN TREE INTO POSITION FOR A ROAD BLOCK. THEY COULD ALREADY HEAR THE SOUND OF MOTOR-ENGINES APPROACHING.

THE MOTOR CYCLE ESCORT TROOPS IMMEDIATELY PULLED UP AND UNSLUNG THEIR SCHMEISSERS, SUSPECTING AN AMBUSH BY FRENCH RESISTANCE FIGHTERS. BUT THE GERMAN GENERAL IN THE STAFF CAR WAS IMPATIENT TO GET ON.

SCHNELL! SCHNELL! CLEAR THE ROAD — DON'T KEEP ME HANGING ABOUT. THE RESISTANCE DOGS WOULDN'T DARE TRY ANYTHING!

BETTER TO CHECK, HERR GENERAL — JUST IN CASE.

BENNY HAD GIVEN THE ORDER NOT TO FIRE UNTIL HE GAVE THE SIGNAL. HE WANTED TO MAKE THE ATTACK AS COMPLETE A SURPRISE AS POSSIBLE, BUT THE TRAP SEEMED ABOUT TO BE REVEALED. BUSTER SWEATED IT OUT AS THE JACK-BOOTED GERMAN FEET CAME CLOSER...

WELL, I CAN'T HELP WHAT THE LIMEY SAYS, I'M GOING TO HAVE TO START SHOOTING IF THIS KRAUT COMES ONE STEP CLOSER.

THAT'S ENOUGH — I CAN'T WAIT HERE ALL DAY. GET THEM BACK — GET THE ROAD CLEAR — WE CAN'T WASTE ANY MORE TIME!

THAT WILL DO. COME BACK AND SHIFT THE TREE. QUICKLY!

AND THE UNCANNY LUCK THAT SEEMED TO GO ALONG WITH EVERYTHING BENNY DID IMPRESSED EVEN THE SCEPTICAL BUSTER.

PHEW, THAT WAS TOO CLOSE FOR COMFORT. THIS ENGLISH CAPTAIN SURE CARRIES GOOD LUCK AROUND WITH HIM.

AND EVEN AS THE ESCORT TROOPS STARTED TO DRAG THE TREE OUT OF THE WAY, BENNY AND DAN WERE GLIDING THROUGH THE UNDERGROWTH TO WITHIN A FEW FEET OF THE STAFF CAR.

GET YOUR HANDS UP, BIG-SHOT.

DO LIKE THE MAN SAYS.

TAKEN COMPLETELY BY SURPRISE THE ESCORT TROOPS GRABBED FOR THEIR SCHMEISSERS. BENNY SHOUTED A QUICK WARNING AS HE BROUGHT UP HIS TOMMY GUN.

DON'T DO IT, MATES. YOU'RE COVERED!

BUT ONE TRIGGER-HAPPY GERMAN IGNORED THE DANGER. HE CUT LOOSE FROM THE HIP IN WILD DEFIANCE, AND A VENOMOUS HAIL OF CROSSFIRE FROM THE HIDDEN AMERICANS SNARLED INTO THE ESCORT TROOPS, DROPPING THEM IN THEIR TRACKS.

WITH THEIR ESCORT DEAD, THE GENERAL, THE JUNIOR OFFICER AND THE DRIVER OF THE STAFF CAR COULD DO NOTHING BUT SURRENDER.

RIGHT. GRAB THE COATS AND HELMETS OFF THESE DEAD JERRIES. I SUPPOSE YOU FOUR CAN RIDE MOTOR-BIKES?

WE SURE CAN, SIR. WE'RE ALL MECHANICS IN THIS OUTFIT. SO FAR WE'VE DONE OK FIGHTING, AND THAT AIN'T OUR JOB. JUST WAIT TILL YOU SEE US HANDLE THEM BIKES!

IT DIDN'T TAKE LONG TO CLEAR THE ROAD, AND SOON THEY WERE READY TO PUSH ON TO LENGRES...AND THE VITAL RADIO.

SAY, CAPTAIN, WHAT ABOUT YOUR TOPCOAT? AIN'T YOU GONNA CHANGE?

NO, I'LL KEEP IT ON. IT — IT'S A GOOD COAT.

BENNY KNEW THAT THE MINUTE HE TOOK OFF THAT COAT HE WOULD BE A CORPORAL AGAIN. HE HAD TO PLAY THE OFFICER ROLE A LITTLE LONGER.

DUMMKOPF. ENGLANDERS — YOU HAVEN'T A CHANCE!

THEY NEVER CHANGE, THE HUNS DON'T!

BUTTON YOUR LIP, KRAUT! BUT YOU BRITISH, YOU SLAY ME. FIRST WE FIND YOU HAVING A QUIET NAP — SLAP IN THE MIDDLE OF A BATTLE, AND NOW YOU'RE GOING TO DRIVE TWENTY MILES THROUGH GERMAN LINES, WEARING BRITISH UNIFORM. OH, BROTHER!

BUT DON'T GET ME WRONG — I'M RIGHT ALONG WITH YOU. I'LL BET YOU'RE DEAD RIGHT — I'D STAKE MY LIFE ON THAT. IT JUST SEEMS A LITTLE PECULIAR, THAT'S ALL. BUT — WHAT THE HECK — I'M JUST A YANK...

AT A HALF-BURNT AMERICAN TRUCK BY THE ROAD-SIDE, THEY STOPPED TO DUMP OFF THEIR UNWANTED PRISONERS.

WE'RE GETTING CLOSE. BETTER PULL THE MOTOR BIKES OUT OF SIGHT OVER THERE. WE'LL NEED TO SEND A SCOUT ON AHEAD.

I'LL GO, BUT WHAT ARE YOU GOING TO DO WITH THE JERRY BRASS-HAT?

BUT EVEN AS BENNY THOUGHT IT OVER, THE FAMILIAR VOICE OF CAPTAIN DUNCAN SOUNDED IN HIS EAR.

HANG ON TO HIM, BENNY — A JERRY GENERAL'S A GOOD HOSTAGE!

WE'LL KEEP HIM AS A HOSTAGE. OK, DAN — YOU GO AND HAVE A LOOK AT THIS VILLAGE. IT'S ABOUT HALF A MILE ALONG THE ROAD. DON'T TAKE ANY CHANCES...AND GET BACK SOON.

LOOK, CAPTAIN, YOU MUST REALISE YOUR POSITION IS HOPELESS. SURRENDER TO ME NOW AND I WILL PERSONALLY SEE THAT YOU AND THE OTHERS ARE ALL WELL TREATED. I GIVE YOU MY WORD AS A GERMAN OFFICER.

QUIET, FRITZ. YOU'RE WASTING YOUR TIME.

BUT BENNY FELT A SUDDEN SHARP TWIST OF MALARIA FEVER, AND FOR THE FIRST TIME DOUBT CREPT INTO HIS MIND. IF HE GAVE UP NOW, AT LEAST THEY'D GET HIM TO A HOSPITAL...

AND DAN'S NEWS, WHEN HE GOT BACK FROM RECONNOITERING THE VILLAGE, ONLY ADDED FUEL TO BENNY'S DOUBTS...

IT'S BAD, SIR — REAL BAD! THEY'VE GOT KRAUTS ALL OVER THE PLACE DOWN THERE, AND IT LOOKS AS IF THEY'RE ROUNDING UP EVERY ABLE-BODIED FRENCHMAN IN THE PLACE! IT'S JUST AS WELL I WAS WEARING THIS GERMAN UNIFORM!

WELL, CAPTAIN? I SEE YOU ARE WAVERING. AS I TOLD YOU, YOUR POSITION IS HOPELESS.

DAN WAS ALL FOR THROWING IN THE TOWEL. THE ODDS SEEMED HOPELESS. BUT THERE WERE THREE VERY IMPORTANT REASONS WHY BENNY COULDN'T GO ALONG WITH HIM.

WELL, BENNY — IS THAT WHAT YOU THINK? THIS IS THE TESTING TIME. WHAT DOES YOUR CONSCIENCE TELL YOU TO DO?

WHAT DO YOU SAY, SIR? LET'S FORGET IT. WE'VE HAD A GOOD RUN. NOBODY COULD BLAME US FOR CALLING QUITS NOW!

WHAT'S IT TO BE THEN, BENNY? DO YOU CARRY ON ....OR ARE YOU JUST LIKE FRED AND ME?

REMEMBER, BENNY — THAT'S AN OFFICER'S COAT YOU'RE WEARING NOW.

AND IN THAT INSTANT BENNY KNEW THAT HE COULD NEVER TURN BACK. HE WAS A BRITISH ARMY CAPTAIN ... AT LEAST IN THE AMERICANS' EYES HE WAS, AND THEY WERE LOOKING TO HIM FOR LEADERSHIP. HE SQUARED HIS SHOULDERS, AND HIS EYES TOOK ON A PURPOSEFUL LOOK —

I WARN YOU, HERR HAUPTMANN. YOU DRIVE TO YOUR DEATH IF YOU SET OFF FOR LENGRES NOW.

WIND IN YOUR NECK, MATE. I GET AWFUL TIRED OF YOUR SQUAWKING! ALL RIGHT, BOYS, DITCH THE JERRY UNIFORMS — THEY WON'T DO YOU ANY GOOD NOW. LET'S GO.

IT WAS NEARLY DUSK WHEN THEY REACHED THE VILLAGE. ON THE OUTSKIRTS, BENNY LEFT DAN WITH THE CAR FOR A QUICK GETAWAY, AND SIGNALLED THE OTHERS TO FOLLOW HIM.

PIERRE SAID THE RADIO WAS IN THE WHITE HOUSE OPPOSITE THE CHURCHYARD. RECKON IT'LL STILL BE THERE?

CAN'T DO WORSE THAN LOOK, DAN. NOW REMEMBER, IF YOU HEAR OUR GUNS POPPING OFF IN A HURRY, COME FAST! OK — BE SEEING YOU!

FROM THEIR HIDING PLACE AMONG THE TOMBSTONES, BENNY AND THE AMERICANS WATCHED AND WAITED. THEY SAW THE FRENCHMEN BEING ROUNDED UP AND HERDED AWAY — AND THEN ONLY THE S.S. TROOPS WERE LEFT ...

LOOKS LIKE THE S.S. ARE STILL GOING STRONG IN THERE.

YEAH, THAT'S GOOD! IT MEANS THEY HAVEN'T FOUND WHAT THEY'RE LOOKING FOR YET.

...AND WHAT THE S.S. WERE LOOKING FOR, WAS IN FACT THE PRECIOUS RADIO.

FOR THE LAST TIME, WOMAN — SPEAK UP! WHERE IS THE RADIO?

I HAVE TOLD YOU, THERE IS NO RADIO. WHAT MORE CAN I SAY?

BUT MEANWHILE, OUTSIDE, ANOTHER S.S. PATROL HAD CAUGHT SIGHT OF THE SHADOWY FIGURES IN THE GRAVE-YARD.

ACHTUNG! WAS IST DEN LOS? HALT, OR I FIRE!

THEY'VE SPOTTED US, BOYS! GIVE 'EM BLAZES!

AND THE AMERICANS SENT A VOLLEY OF SCHMEISSER LEAD SNARLING INTO THE GERMANS.

THE S.S. MEN INSIDE THE HOUSE DASHED TO THE WINDOW AT THE SOUND OF FIRING OUTSIDE.

MEIN GOTT! WE ARE BEING ATTACKED. WHAT IS HAPPENING OUT THERE?

ONLY A SKIRMISH WITH THE FRENCH SCHWEINHUNDS, NO DOUBT. WE HAVE NO CAUSE TO WORRY IN HERE.

BUT EVEN AS THEY TURNED BACK TO THE OLD WOMAN, THE DOOR SUDDENLY CRASHED OPEN, AND BENNY WALKER BURST INTO THE ROOM, TOMMY GUN BLAZING.

MON DIEU! AN ENGLISHMAN! THANK HEAVEN YOU HAVE COME ...MON PAUVRE FILS, MY POOR SON IS —

QUICK, THE RADIO! WHERE'S THE RADIO?

THE S.S. MEN LAY DEAD ONLY INCHES FROM THE SECRET RADIO THEY HAD TRIED SO HARD TO FIND.

IT IS HERE, MY BOY, SAFE AND SOUND...

THERE'S NO TIME TO LOSE! I'VE GOT TO TRANSMIT A MESSAGE.

AND AS BENNY STARTED RELAYING THE CODED INFORMATION BACK, EXCITEMENT BUZZED AT H.Q.

RADIO "LIEUTENANT" MAKING CONTACT, SIR.

"LIEUTENANT" THAT'S PIERRE'S OUTFIT. JUST WHEN WE'D GIVEN HIM UP FOR LOST. NOW WE'RE GETTING SOMEWHERE.

THANK HEAVEN — NOT A MINUTE TOO SOON!

AND THOUGH THE STAFF OFFICERS AT H.Q. WERE PUZZLED BY THE IDENTITY OF THEIR INFORMANT, THEY SOON GOT TO WORK ON THE INFORMATION RECEIVED.

WELL, IT'S ALL HERE! FUNNY THOUGH — WHO WAS IT ON THE OTHER END? NOT A FRENCHMAN, WAS HE?

NO, ENGLISH. CHAP CALLED WALKER. DON'T UNDERSTAND IT, REALLY. CAPTAIN DUNCAN WAS OUR LIAISON, BUT NOTHING'S BEEN HEARD OF HIM. STILL, THE CODE'S RIGHT AND WE'VE GOT THE INFO NOW.

AND AS SOON AS THE GENERAL HEARD THE DETAILS OF THE STRENGTH OF THE GERMAN COUNTER-ATTACK, HE ALTERED HIS PLANS ACCORDINGLY.

IT SOUNDS AS THOUGH JERRY'S RISKING EVERYTHING ON A QUICK BREAK-THROUGH. BUT WE'LL BE READY FOR HIM, BY JOVE! WE'LL MOVE UP HERE — AND HERE, AND WE'LL BE WAITING TO KNOCK HIM FOR SIX!

THERE'S A BIT OF A MYSTERY ABOUT WHO SENT THE REPORT, SIR. HE WAS ONE OF OUR CHAPS ALL RIGHT, BUT NOT THE MAN WHO WAS LIAISON WITH THE RESISTANCE.

WELL, WHOEVER IT WAS PUT UP A DASHED FINE SHOW — A DASHED FINE SHOW!

YES, SIR — I'LL GET THESE ORDERS POSTED NOW, SIR. OUR ARMOUR WILL BE MOVING NORTH WITHIN THE HOUR.

MEANWHILE, BENNY HAD TRANSMITTED THE INFORMATION AND WAS ALL SET FOR A QUICK GETAWAY. BUT THE OLD FRENCHWOMAN FOLLOWED HIM FROM THE HOUSE.

BUT MY SON, AND THE OTHER MEN — YOU MUST SAVE THEM!

HAVE A HEART, MOTHER! I CAN'T FIGHT THE WHOLE PERISHING GERMAN ARMY ON MY OWN.

THEN SUDDENLY A FUSILLADE OF BULLETS WHIZZED PAST.

GET DOWN! GET DOWN!

BUT MY SON — PLEASE HELP HIM AND THE OTHERS.

THIS IS YOUR CHANCE TO MAKE UP FOR THOSE PRISONERS I LEFT IN THE LURCH BACK IN 1917. SAVE THEM, BENNY — FOR THEIR OWN SAKES — AND FOR ME!

OK, MOTHER ... I'LL HAVE A BASH!

THE SOUND OF GUN-FIRE HAD BROUGHT THE STAFF-
CAR WITH DAN AT THE WHEEL, RACING UP THE STREET.
IT SCREECHED TO A HALT AS BENNY AND THE FOUR
AMERICANS CAME RUNNING TOWARDS IT.

ALL ABOARD. MAKE
IT SNAPPY, BOYS. THE
AIR AIN'T TOO HEALTHY
ABOUT HERE!

WHERE
ARE WE GOING,
SIR?

TO THE RAILWAY.
THAT'S IT AT THE
OTHER END OF THE
VILLAGE.

BUT BEFORE THEY REACHED THE STATION, BENNY
CAUGHT SIGHT OF A SIGNAL BOX. QUICKLY HE
TOLD DAN TO PULL UP ALONGSIDE.

RIGHT, DAN. YOU AND BUSTER GET
CONTROL OF THE SIGNAL BOX. AND MAKE
THE SIGNALMAN STOP THE TRAIN JUST BEFORE
IT GETS HERE. THE REST OF US WILL UNHITCH
THE TRUCK WITH THE PRISONERS IN IT.

OK, SIR.
WE'LL FIX IT!

GEE! IF ANYBODY HAD TOLD
ME YESTERDAY I'D BE DOING A JESSE
JAMES, STICKING UP RAILROAD CARS
— I'D HAVE SAID HE WAS LOCO!

THE TRAIN WAS TRUNDLING DOWN THE LINE TOWARDS THEM, AND SLOWLY PICKING UP SPEED AS DAN AND BUSTER DISAPPEARED INSIDE THE SIGNAL BOX. THEN SUDDENLY, THE SIGNAL CLANGED DOWN, AND WITH A TORTURED HISSING AND SQUEALING THE TRAIN SHUDDERED TO A STOP.

OK — THAT'S IT. SIGNAL DAN TO LET 'EM GO AGAIN.

SURE! I'LL SET 'EM OFF!

IT WAS THE WORK OF SECONDS FOR BENNY AND THE G.I.'S TO UNCOUPLE THE LAST TRUCK.

SLOWLY THE TRAIN MOVED OFF, BUT BENNY REALISED THE GERMANS WOULD SOON SEE SOMETHING WAS WRONG.

THEY'LL BE BACK SOON ENOUGH. YOU LOT GET READY TO HOLD 'EM OFF WHILE I GET THIS WAGON OPENED.

ALL THIS WHILE, THE NAZI GENERAL HAD BEEN LYING BOUND AND GAGGED IN THE STOLEN STAFF CAR.

THE HOSTAGE, BENNY! GET THE GENERAL TO USE AS AS A HOSTAGE.

QUICK! GET THE JERRY BRASS-HAT AND FETCH HIM HERE!

BENNY STARTED TO FORCE THE WAGON DOORS, BUT UP AHEAD, THE TRAIN HAD STOPPED AGAIN.

THEY'VE STOPPED THE TRAIN, SIR. THEY'RE COMING BACK FOR US.

HOLD 'EM OFF! HOLD 'EM OFF TILL I GET THESE BLOKES OUT!

BUT THE WAGON DOOR HELD FIRM, AND BY NOW THE GERMANS WERE ADVANCING STEADILY, FIRING AS THEY CAME.

HOLY SMOKE! AM I NEVER GOING TO GET THIS OPEN?

KEEP AT IT, BENNY! DON'T GIVE UP. DON'T GIVE UP, BENNY — I ONCE DID!

THEN SUDDENLY THE DOORS GAVE.

AT LAST! COME ON, MATES! OUT YOU GET!

IT'S ALL OVER, SIR. WE'RE JUST ABOUT OUT OF AMMO. DO WE MAKE A RUN FOR IT?

NO ... AT LEAST, NOT UNTIL I GET THE JERRIES TO HOLD THEIR FIRE. I'LL TAKE THE GENERAL IN UNDER A WHITE FLAG. THE FRENCHIES'LL TAKE CARE OF YOU.

BUT — BUT YOU CAN'T JUST GIVE YOURSELF UP, SIR.

BENNY SMILED WEARILY AS HE STEPPED OUT OF COVER AND PRODDED THE GERMAN TOWARDS HIS OWN MEN —

AND WHY NOT? IF I GO BACK TO OUR OWN MOB, I'LL PROBABLY HAVE TO FACE A COURT-MARTIAL FOR IMPERSONATING A SENIOR OFFICER IN ANY CASE. YOU SEE I'M ONLY A CORPORAL MECHANIC. DON'T WORRY BOYS — I KNOW WHAT I'M DOING.

WELL, STRIKE ME PINK! HE — HE AIN'T AN OFFICER AT ALL!

Y'KNOW, I REALLY THINK HE WANTS US TO LET HIM GO. IF EVER I SAW A GUY WITH A MISSION, IT'S THAT LIMEY — LET'S HOPE HE MAKES IT!

AND AS BENNY AND HIS PRISONER WALKED TOWARDS THE GERMAN POSITIONS, THE G.I.'S AND THE FRENCHMEN SLIPPED AWAY IN THE DARKNESS.

YOU'LL NEVER GET AWAY WITH IT.

WE HAVE ALREADY. YOUR MOB ARE HOLDING FIRE TO SAVE YOUR SKIN, AND THAT'S GIVEN US ENOUGH TIME FOR THE REST TO GET AWAY, GENERAL.

AND IN A DESPERATE BID TO SAVE FACE — THE GENERAL SUDDENLY GRABBED FOR BENNY'S TOMMY GUN...

YOU HAVE TRIED TO MAKE A FOOL OF ME, ENGLISH PIG. NOW YOU WILL SUFFER ....AAAGH....

BUT AS THE GENERAL FELL, THE GERMANS OPENED FIRE AGAIN, AND BENNY MADE HIS LAST DEFIANT STAND.

COME ON, THEN! COME ON! LET'S HAVE YOU, JERRY-BOYS!

THERE COULD BE NO ESCAPE, AND BENNY — HIS TASK ACCOMPLISHED — WOULD HAVE WANTED NONE. HIS LIFELESS FINGER WAS STILL PRESSED HARD ON THE TOMMY GUN TRIGGER, AS HIS KNEES BUCKLED SLOWLY BENEATH HIM.

AND NOW BENNY WAS NO LONGER ALONE. A HERO'S WELCOME AWAITED HIM, BEYOND THAT SHELL-SCORCHED PLACE...

WELL DONE, BENNY WALKER. YOU'VE BEEN A CREDIT TO US ALL. WELCOME HOME, MATE!

THANKS, SIR ... THANKS FOR ALL THE HELP.

NOW TOMMY THOMPSON AND FRED BOWLING WERE FREE TO REST. THEY HAD ATONED THROUGH THE BRAVERY OF ANOTHER MAN FOR THEIR OWN PERSONAL FAILURES.

MY HUMBLEST GRATITUDE, BENNY. YOU GOT THROUGH WITH THE DISPATCHES. GOD BLESS YOU!

AND THE PRISONERS GOT AWAY. YOU MADE UP FOR ME TOO, BENNY. YOU'RE A VERY BRAVE MAN.

KNOCK IT OFF, BOYS. I COULDN'T HAVE DONE ANY OF IT WITHOUT YOUR HELP. THIS WAS A TEAM JOB ... WE ALL DID OUR BIT.

AND SO IN DEATH THEY WERE UNITED — FOUR MEN WHO HAD FOUGHT AND DIED IN THE MUD OF FLANDERS IN THREE DIFFERENT WARS. YET EVEN IN DEATH THEY HAD WON THROUGH TO VICTORY. AND FOR TROOPER FRED BOWLING AND PTE. TOMMY THOMSON, THAT VICTORY MEANT THEY COULD AT LAST REST IN PEACE...

Commando
THE END

NIGHT OF FEAR

Transylvania — an eerie land of legends, of werewolves and vampires, of hauntings and spine-chilling screams in the dark.

Not the most welcoming place in the world to crash-land in at dead of night — especially when your Mosquito is damaged, not by Nazi ack-ack...but by a swarm of millions of large, black bats!

Commando
THE SILVER COLLECTION

www.commandocomics.com

COMPLETE 63-PAGE ACTION STORY

Commando

THE SILVER COLLECTION

WAR IN EUROPE 1939-45

NIGHT OF FEAR

Story: Alan Hebden
Born in Bristol in 1950, Alan Hebden decided to follow the footsteps of his father, prolific *Commando* writer and army major, Eric Hebden, and pursue work in comics. Hebden's career began by writing scripts for *Commando*, *Victor*, and *Hornet*, then for Fleetway's *Battle Picture Weekly*, *Tornado*, *Starlord* and *2000 AD*. Look out for further *Commando Presents* featuring Alan's work!

Art: Patrick Wright
Patrick Wright, also known as Pat Wright, worked heavily in the British Comics industry. Wright followed the legacy of his father, David Wright, another comic artist and creator of *Carol Day* for the *Daily Mail*. Like his father, Wright worked for DC Thomson, but the younger focussed his work on *Commando*. Wright also worked for DC Thomson's rival Fleetway on *Battle Picture Weekly*, *Eagle* and *2000 AD*. Patrick is well known for his work on *Modesty Blaise*.

Cover: Ian Kennedy
One of the most beloved artists in all of *Commando's* history, Ian Kennedy was born in Dundee in 1932. Kennedy was employed by D. C. Thomson & Co., working as a trainee illustrator in their Art Department in 1949, while also attending courses at the Dundee College of Art. His first published work was inking the black squares in the weekly *Sunday Post* crossword. In 1953, Kennedy left to work for Amalgamated Press, before returning to D. C. Thomson again in 1955 as a freelance artist. His credits included work on such titles as *Warlord, The Hotspur, Victor, The Hornet, Starblazer* and, of course, *Commando*. Ian continued to provide covers for *Commando* until sadly passing in 2022. His legacy and outstanding contribution to British comics is undeniable!

NIGHT OF FEAR

TRANSYLVANIA...A NAME INTERWOVEN WITH LEGEND AND MYSTERY FOR SO LONG THAT TO MANY IT IS NOTHING MORE THAN A FANCIFUL SETTING FOR TALES OF VAMPIRES AND WEREWOLVES. YET TRANSYLVANIA IS REAL ENOUGH — A PROVINCE OF RUMANIA, REMOTE AND DISTANT PERHAPS, BUT NOT ENOUGH TO HAVE ESCAPED THE SAVAGE STRUGGLE OF THE SECOND WORLD WAR.

IN THE AUTUMN OF 1943 RUMANIA WAS STILL NOMINALLY AN ALLY OF NAZI GERMANY, BUT NOT ALL RUMANIANS WERE WILLING TO SIT BACK QUIETLY AND ACCEPT THE EVER-INCREASING BURDENS GERMANY WAS FORCING THEIR COUNTRY TO ACCEPT.

THAT'S ANOTHER LOT OF OIL THE HUNS WILL NOT TAKE FROM OUR LAND.

ACHTUNG... SABOTEURS!

THE ANTI-NAZI PARTISANS HIT BACK HARD WHEN AND WHERE THEY COULD. EVEN THE LUFTWAFFE WERE NOT SAFE.

QUICKLY, BACK TO THE MOUNTAINS. WE HAVE DONE WHAT WE CAME TO DO.

AS RESISTANCE BECAME MORE WIDESPREAD, THE GERMANS CALLED IN S.S. GENERAL LUDWIG VON STACH, AN ELEGANT BUT RUTHLESS MAN WHOSE NAME SPELLED TERROR THROUGHOUT THE OCCUPIED LANDS OF EASTERN EUROPE.

WHAT IS THIS PLACE, MAJOR POEST?

THE CASTLE REMPAVI, HERR GENERAL. IT BELONGS TO THE OLD COUNT REMPAVI. HE'S SOMETHING OF A HERMIT. BIT OF A NATUR- ALIST TOO — STUDIES BATS, I BELIEVE.

BATS? THE GENERAL SNORTED. SOME PEOPLE OBVIOUSLY DIDN'T KNOW THERE WAS A WAR ON.

VON STACH'S ANTI-GUERILLA FORCE WAS OUT TO CRUSH THE PARTISANS, BUT THE LAST FEW DAYS HAD YIELDED NOTHING. THE CASTLE WOULD DO FOR A FEW HOURS' RELAXATION.

IS ANYBODY THERE? OPEN THESE GATES!

MY MASTER SEES NO ONE. WHO ARE YOU?

THAT BROUGHT A VERY ANGRY REPLY. VON STACH WAS NOT USED TO BEING TREATED THIS WAY.

GENERAL VON STACH OF THE S.S., AND I DEMAND ENTRY. IF THESE GATES ARE NOT OPEN IN TWO MINUTES I'LL HAVE THEM BLASTED TO PIECES!

NO, NO... WAIT! I MUST ASK MY MASTER!

VON STACH'S DEADLINE HAD JUST EXPIRED WHEN THE GATES CREAKED OPEN, PUSHED BY A POWERFUL HUNCHBACK.

MY MASTER BIDS YOU WELCOME.

NOT A MOMENT TOO SOON EITHER. ANOTHER FEW SECONDS AND HE WOULD HAVE BEEN BIDDING ME WELCOME WHETHER HE LIKED IT OR NOT. TAKE ME TO HIM IMMEDIATELY.

COUNT REMPAVI WAS WAITING IN THE COURTYARD.

HE SAYS HE IS GENERAL VON STACH OF THE S.S., MASTER.

ARE YOU SUGGESTING I AM AN IMPOSTER, OAF?

THE COUNT SMILED, SHOWING STARTINGLY WHITE TEETH.

FORGIVE ZABA — HE DOES NOT CARE MUCH FOR STRANGERS. YOU ARE WELCOME HERE. PLEASE HAVE DINNER WITH ME.

THIS INVITATION PUT THE GENERAL IN A BETTER FRAME OF MIND, AS DID THE EXCELLENT MEAL SERVED BY ZABA.

THE COUNT SMILED SLIGHTLY AS HE REPLIED.

A FINE DINNER, COUNT. IT IS GOOD TO FIND THAT NOT ALL OUR ALLIES ARE DESERTING US BECAUSE OF A FEW SETBACKS.

THE WAR MEANS LITTLE TO ME, GENERAL, SO LONG AS IT DOES NOT INTERFERE WITH MY LIFE HERE.

VON STACH DID NOT APPROVE OF THIS ATTITUDE.

YOU CANNOT BURY YOUR HEAD IN THE SAND LIKE AN OSTRICH. RUMANIA IS OUR ALLY. YOU SUPPLY US WITH OIL, AND WE GRANT YOU THE PROTECTION OF THE THIRD REICH.

FROM WHAT I HEAR, NOT ALL MY COUNTRYMEN WOULD AGREE WITH YOU THERE. NOT THAT SUCH THINGS CONCERN ME . . .

THE GENERAL'S AIDE, MAJOR POEST, INTERVENED.

THEN IT OUGHT TO CONCERN YOU — ESPECIALLY AS YOUR CASTLE IS IN THE MOUNTAINS WHERE THESE REBELS OPERATE. WE HAVE HEARD THAT YOUR SON MAY BE INVOLVED.

MY SON? YOU MUST BE MISTAKEN!

BUT IT WAS TIME FOR THE GERMANS TO RETURN TO THEIR BASE MUCH FURTHER DOWN THE VALLEY. VON STACH HAD A LAST WORD OF ADVICE FOR THE OLD COUNT—

IF YOUR SON IS MIXED UP WITH THE GUERILLAS, I ADVISE YOU TO PERSUADE HIM TO GIVE IT UP. IF HE SHOULD FALL INTO MY HANDS I WOULD BE OBLIGED TO MAKE AN EXAMPLE OF HIM.

I HAVE ALREADY TOLD YOU YOUR SUSPICIONS ARE UNFOUNDED. GOODBYE, GENERAL. FEEL FREE TO VISIT ME. YOU WILL ALWAYS BE WELCOME.

THE GERMANS DISAPPEARED DOWN THE VALLEY AND THE COUNT RETURNED TO THE MAIN HALL, WHERE BRADU, HIS SON, APPEARED FROM BEHIND A TAPESTRY.

I HOPE YOU HEARD WHAT THE GERMANS SAID. IF YOU INSIST ON TAKING THESE FOOLISH RISKS AND THEY CATCH YOU, THEN EXPECT NO HELP FROM ME.

THAT'S THE LAST THING I'D EXPECT FROM YOU, FATHER. THE GERMAN WAS RIGHT — YOU ARE LIKE AN OSTRICH. WE ARE NOT ALLIES OF GERMANY, WE ARE SLAVES WHO LET THEM STEAL OUR OIL! DON'T YOU CARE AT ALL?

BRADU KNEW THE ANSWER BEFORE HE ASKED. THE COUNT'S WORDS CAME AS NO SURPRISE.

THE WAR IS OF NO CONCERN TO ME. BUT JUST REMEMBER YOU ARE PLAYING A DANGEROUS GAME. ZABA, PREPARE MY BED.

AT LEAST SOME OF US CARE FOR RUMANIA'S FUTURE! I'LL FIGHT THE NAZIS TO MY LAST BREATH IF NEED BE, AND YOU'D BETTER REALISE THAT, FATHER!

EVEN AS COUNT REMPAVI WENT WEARILY TO HIS BED, AN R.A.F. MOSQUITO WAS COMING IN TO LAND AT A RECENTLY CAPTURED AIRFIELD IN ITALY AFTER A RECCE FLIGHT ACROSS GERMAN LINES TO THE NORTH.

FLIGHT-LIEUTENANT HOWARD GARFORTH AND FLYING-OFFICER JOHN KNOWLES WERE THE CREW. ON THIS PARTICULAR EVENING JOHN KNOWLES SEEMED UNUSUALLY EAGER TO GET BACK ON TIME. ALMOST BEFORE THEY'D STOPPED ROLLING, HE WAS OUT OF HIS STRAPS.

HOWARD LAUGHED. THE WHOLE SQUADRON KNEW ABOUT JOHN'S OBSESSION WITH HORROR FILMS AND BOOKS.

HAVEN'T SEEN MISTER KNOWLES MOVE SO FAST FOR AGES, SIR. COULDN'T BE ANYTHING TO DO WITH THAT FILM THEY'RE SHOWING TONIGHT, COULD IT?

I DON'T KNOW WHAT YOU MEAN, SMITHY.

NOT EVERYONE WAS AMUSED BY JOHN'S ENTHUSIASM. IN THEIR SHARED TENT THEIR BATMAN HAD A PROBLEM.

NOT MORE VAMPIRE COMICS — I THREW OUT ABOUT A HUNDRED YESTERDAY!

BLAME THE YANKS. THEY FLY A PLANE-LOAD IN EVERY WEEK.

LATER HOWARD MET JOHN COMING OUT OF THE FILM TENT.

YOU MISSED A GREAT FILM. I WONDER IF TRANSYLVANIA REALLY LOOKS LIKE THAT?

NOT IF IT WAS MADE IN HOLLY-WOOD. NEVER MIND, MAYBE YOU CAN VISIT IT AFTER THE WAR. YOU WON'T GET THE CHANCE BEFORE THEN.

BUT HOWARD WAS WRONG. FAR AWAY IN MOSCOW A TOP-LEVEL COMMITTEE WAS MEETING BEHIND THE RAMPARTS OF THE KREMLIN.

IT IS ESSENTIAL WE DIVERT BOMBERS FROM THEIR ATTACKS ON THE RUMANIAN OILFIELDS. BUT THIS WILL LEAVE THE GERMANS FREE TO INCREASE THEIR OIL PRODUCTION AND PERHAPS PRO-LONG THE WAR. WHAT CAN YOU SUGGEST, MISTER CHAIRMAN?

THE BRITISH AND AMERICANS HAVE BOMBER FORCES STATIONED IN SOUTHERN ITALY, WELL WITHIN RANGE OF THE OIL-FIELDS. I WILL ASK THEM TO HELP...

A WEEK LATER THAT STRATEGIC DECISION HAD FILTERED THROUGH TO THE MEN WHO WOULD HAVE TO CARRY IT OUT. AT A BRIEFING THEIR NEW TARGET WAS EXPLAINED — A TARGET THAT DELIGHTED JOHN KNOWLES.

IT'LL BE UP TO YOU PATHFINDERS TO PINPOINT THE OIL-WELLS AT LOW-LEVEL FOR THE MAIN FORCE. THEY'RE SITUATED IN THE FOOT-HILLS OF THE TRANSYLVANIAN ALPS, SO DON'T GO HITTING ANY MOUNTAINSIDES, OK?

TRANSYLVANIA! AT LAST I'LL BE ABLE TO SEE IT FOR MYSELF.

THEY WERE READY TO GO AT SUNSET, THOUGH JOHN RECEIVED A COUPLE OF LIGHT-HEARTED WARNINGS.

WATCH OUT FOR LOW-FLYING VAMPIRE BATS, KNOWLESY. I HEAR THEY'RE PRETTY ACTIVE ROUND MIDNIGHT.

AND DON'T TAKE ANY BLOOD FROM STRANGERS.

VERY FUNNY... I DON'T THINK.

AS THEY PREPARED FOR TAKE-OFF, JOHN FUMBLED IN HIS JACKET.

NOT MORE VAMPIRE COMICS, FOR PETE'S SAKE!

IF WE GET SHOT DOWN I CAN USE THEM AS GUIDE-BOOKS...

A FEW HOURS LATER THE GERMANS AT THE PLOESTI OILFIELD BRACED THEM-SELVES FOR ANOTHER RAID.

FROM THE SOUTH-WEST TONIGHT. IT'S THE ACCURSED R.A.F.

TAKING A NIGHT OFF FROM HAMBURG, EH? BETTER SOUND THE ALARM...

THE SIRENS HAD BARELY SOUNDED BEFORE THE PATHFINDING MOSQUITOES ARRIVED, LED BY HOWARD AND JOHN.

WELL, WHAT DO YOU THINK OF RUMANIA?

NOT MUCH SO FAR. LET'S THROW A BIT OF LIGHT ON THE SCENE.

AS THE MOSQUITO UNLOADED ITS INCENDIARY BOMBS AND FLARES, THE TARGET WAS BATHED IN A LURID GLARE.

SMACK ON THE NOSE. THOSE BOMBER CREWS WILL HAVE TO BE BLIND TO MISS THAT.

THE BOMBER CREWS WEREN'T BLIND, AND SOON THE OILFIELD WAS A MASSIVE INFERNO OF HUGE FIRES AND EXPLOSIONS...THOUGH JOHN SCARCELY NOTICED.

NICE WORK. THERE WON'T BE MUCH LEFT HERE BY MORNING.

THOSE MUST BE THE TRANSYLVANIAN ALPS OVER THERE. HEY, WHAT ABOUT A SPIN OVER THE MOUNTAINS? I'D LOVE TO HAVE A CLOSE LOOK AT THE REAL THING.

SUCH A DETOUR WAS STRICTLY AGAINST ORDERS, BUT SOME OF JOHN'S ENTHUSIASM HAD RUBBED OFF ON HOWARD. SO, A FEW MINUTES LATER —

LOOK AT THAT CASTLE — STRAIGHT OUT OF THAT FILM. GET IN CLOSER.

MAKE THE MOST OF IT, WE'VE ONLY GOT TWO MINUTES NOW.

THE SOUND OF THE AIRCRAFT BROUGHT THE COUNT AND HIS SON TO THE BATTLEMENTS.

IT'S AN R.A.F. PLANE! WHAT ARE THEY DOING HERE?

I DON'T KNOW, AND I WISH THEY'D GO AWAY. THEY'LL UPSET MY BATS.

THE PLANE TURNED STEEPLY FOR ANOTHER RUN OVER THE CASTLE.

THEY'RE COMING BACK. WHAT WOULDN'T I GIVE TO BE ABLE TO BE WITH THEM.

THEY'RE FOOLS OR MADMEN. HAVEN'T THEY SEEN THE BATS YET!

THE COUNT WAS FURIOUS. DISTURBED BY THE NOISE OF THE MERLIN ENGINES, THOUSANDS OF HIS BATS WERE FLYING OUT OF THE TOWER WHERE THEY LIVED — STRAIGHT INTO THE PATH OF THE MOSQUITO.

BLACK BATS AT NIGHT WEREN'T THE EASIEST THING TO SPOT, AND WHEN JOHN EVENTUALLY SAW THEM IT WAS TOO LATE TO DO ANYTHING.

HOLY SMOKE, BATS — HUNDREDS OF THEM! WHERE DID THEY COME FROM?

FROM YOUR BLASTED CASTLE, THAT'S WHERE!

FOR THE AIRMEN THE JOY-RIDE TURNED SWIFTLY INTO A NIGHTMARE AS THEY HURTLED INTO THE SWARM. THE TWO WATCHED IN HORROR FROM THE CASTLE.

THEY HAVE COLLIDED WITH THE BATS! THEY ARE SURELY DOOMED.

THEY'RE GOING TO CRASH NEAR THE VILLAGE ACROSS THE RIDGE. I MUST SEE IF THEY HAVE SURVIVED OR NOT.

ONCE BRADU HAD MADE UP HIS MIND NOTHING COULD STOP HIM. SOON HE WAS SETTING OUT, MUCH TO HIS FATHER'S DISGUST.

AS YOU INSIST ON THIS MAD HUNT FOR A COUPLE OF STUPID PILOTS WHO ARE PROBABLY DEAD BY NOW ANYWAY, I FORBID YOU TO BRING THEM BACK HERE, SHOULD YOU FIND THEM ALIVE.

AND WHAT WOULD YOU DO, FATHER? LOCK US UP AND CALL VON STACH? I SHALL DO WHAT I MUST, AND DON'T TRY TO STOP ME.

THE COUNT SHOOK HIS HEAD AS HE WATCHED HIS SON RIDE OFF INTO THE NIGHT. BESIDE HIM THE FAITHFUL ZABA SIGHED. IT WAS BAD ENOUGH THAT BRADU DISOBEYED HIS FATHER, BUT WITH NAZIS AROUND IT WAS TEN TIMES WORSE.

MEANWHILE THE TWO AIRMEN HAD ABANDONED THEIR DOOMED PLANE.

WE'RE IN LUCK. THERE'S A CLEARING BELOW, AND NO SIGN OF THE JERRIES YET, EITHER.

THEY LANDED SAFELY AND HID THEIR PARACHUTES. JOHN WAS STILL CHUCKLING AS HE PULLED OUT A MAP.

I STILL DON'T BELIEVE IT . . . DOWNED BY BATS OVER TRANSYLVANIA. HOW VERY APPROPRIATE! MIND YOU, I'M NOT SURE HOW WE'LL GET HOME . . .

OH, SHUT UP! IT'S NO LAUGHING MATTER. YOU GOT US INTO THIS— NOW GET US OUT!

THEY FOUND A ROAD AND BEGAN WALKING, BUT SHORTLY AFTERWARDS —

SOMETHING'S COMING!

QUICKLY, INTO THE BUSHES.

IT WAS VON STACH'S ANTI-GUERILLA FORCE, TEMPORARILY ON THE SCENT OF A NEW QUARRY.

SCHNELL, SCHNELL...THE BRITISH AIRCRAFT CRASHED ONLY A FEW KILOMETRES FROM HERE.

WOW, THEY'VE SENT A GENERAL AFTER US. WE'D BETTER GET MOVING AS SOON AS IT'S CLEAR.

THEY SET OFF AGAIN AS SOON AS THE GERMANS HAD DISAPPEARED AND SOON CAME TO A SMALL VILLAGE.

WE MUST BE RIGHT IN THE MIDDLE OF VAMPIRE COUNTRY BY NOW, AND THAT MUST BE THE VILLAGE INN.

IT'S THE ONLY BUILDING THAT LOOKS INHABITED. WE'LL HAVE TO SOUND OUT THE INNKEEPER. IF HE TURNS US IN, THAT'S OUR BAD LUCK. COME ON.

THE SIGHT OF THE TWO R.A.F. AIRCREW NEARLY GAVE THE INNKEEPER A HEART ATTACK, BUT...

BRITISH PILOTS, HERE? COME IN, QUICKLY. BUT NO ONE MUST SEE YOU.

THANKS A MILLION.

THE INNKEEPER WAS NO GUERILLA, BUT HE HAD LITTLE LOVE FOR THE GERMANS.

IT IS NOT SAFE TO STAY HERE, BUT I KNOW PEOPLE WHO CAN HELP. MY SON WILL GO AND TELL THEM.

YOU'RE ALREADY DOING MORE THAN WE COULD HAVE HOPED FOR.

AFTER THE BOY HAD GONE THE INNKEEPER GAVE THEM SOME FOOD. BUT IT WAS THE INN ITSELF THAT FASCINATED JOHN.

LOOK AT ALL THAT GARLIC STRUNG AROUND THE PLACE. ACCORDING TO LEGEND, IT WARDS OFF VAMPIRES. I'LL BET THAT'S WHY IT'S HERE.

WHY DON'T YOU ASK THE INN- KEEPER ABOUT IT?

JOHN ASKED ABOUT THE GARLIC, AND WAS ASTONISHED AS THE INNKEEPER ROARED WITH LAUGHTER.

YOU MEAN IT'S NOT FOR KEEPING AWAY EVIL SPIRITS?

EVIL SPIRITS? HA, HA, I'VE HEARD OF YOU PEOPLE BELIEVING THAT RUBBISH. YOU AMAZE ME. NO, THE GARLIC KEEPS BEST THAT WAY, THAT'S ALL.

HOWARD COULD NOT RESIST A JIBE AS JOHN RETURNED MOROSELY TO HIS MEAL.

SO WHAT HAPPENED TO THE YOKELS LIVING IN DREAD AFTER THE SUN SETS, EH?

MUST BE IN THE WRONG PART OF THE COUNTRY, THAT'S ALL.

MEANWHILE THE INNKEEPER'S SON HAD RUN INTO BRADU.

BRADU, MY FATHER SENT ME. TWO BRITISH PILOTS ARE AT THE INN.

WHAT LUCK! TAKE ME TO THEM, QUICKLY.

BRADU TOOK CHARGE AS SOON AS HE ARRIVED.

COME WITH ME. I AM A MEMBER OF THE LOCAL RESISTANCE. I WILL KEEP YOU HIDDEN UNTIL I CAN ARRANGE TRANSPORT FOR YOU.

THANK YOU FOR EVERYTHING, SIR.

DODGING ALONG NARROW, HIDDEN TRAILS THAT HE KNEW LIKE THE BACK OF HIS HAND, BRADU LED THEM BACK TO THE GLOOMY CASTLE.

THIS IS MY FATHER'S CASTLE. HE IS COUNT REMPAVI AND HE IS UNLIKELY TO BE OVER-JOYED TO SEE YOU. BUT FEAR NOT, HE WILL SAY NOTHING.

IT'S THE CASTLE WE BUZZED BEFORE SMASHING INTO THE BATS. IT LOOKS EVEN BETTER FROM GROUND LEVEL – STRAIGHT OUT OF A HORROR FILM.

BRADU CHUCKLED.

OH, YES — BEFORE THE WAR SEVERAL SUCH FILMS WERE MADE HERE ABOUT THE VAMPIRE LEGEND — NOT THAT ANYONE BELIEVES IT TODAY, OF COURSE.

OF COURSE. WHO WOULD POSSIBLY BELIEVE ANYTHING LIKE THAT?

ALL RIGHT, ALL RIGHT...I HEARD YOU.

AS BRADU HAD PREDICTED, THE COUNT WAS FAR FROM HAPPY WHEN HE SAW THE GUESTS.

I TOLD YOU NOT TO BRING THEM HERE. IF THE GERMANS FIND THEM, WE ARE ALL LOST.

IF NO ONE SPEAKS, THE GERMANS WILL NOT FIND THEM, FATHER. THEY'LL ONLY BE HERE FOR AS LONG AS IT TAKES TO ARRANGE TRANSPORT. FIND THEM A ROOM WHILE I DO THAT.

THEY FOLLOWED THE SURLY HUNCHBACK THROUGH THE CASTLE TO A LUXURIOUS BEDROOM.

YOU STAY HERE. NOT LEAVE. PULL BELL-ROPE IF YOU WANT ANYTHING.

WE'D HAVE BEEN WORSE OFF AT THE RITZ.

AND THE SINISTER MANSERVANT LEFT THEM ALONE.

SPOOKY BLOKE, THAT COUNT. BRADU WAS RIGHT ABOUT HIM NOT WANTING US, NOT THAT I BLAME HIM. AT LEAST WE'RE SAFE AND COMFORTABLE FOR THE MOMENT.

ALL I CAN SAY IS THAT IF PEOPLE WHO LIVE IN THIS CASTLE DON'T BELIEVE IN VAMPIRES, THEN WHAT HOPE CAN THERE BE FOR THE WORLD? I'M GLAD I BROUGHT THESE COMICS ALONG NOW, EVEN IF THEY WON'T BE QUITE THE SAME AGAIN.

THEIR CONVERSATION MASKED THE SLIGHT SOUND OF A KEY TURNING IN THE WELL-OILED LOCK AS ZABA FOLLOWED HIS MASTER'S INSTRUCTIONS.

GRIMLY THE SINISTER HUNCHBACK LIMPED OFF DOWN THE CORRIDOR.

DON'T LET THEM WANDER ROUND, THE MASTER SAID. WELL, THEY WON'T GET OUT OF THERE IN A HURRY...

IN THE VILLAGE THE GERMANS HAD ARRIVED AT THE INN AFTER A FRUITLESS SEARCH.

WELCOME TO MY HUMBLE INN, GENTLEMEN.

FETCH US COFFEE AND SCHNAPPS, AND BE QUICK ABOUT IT. MY TEMPER IS SHORT AFTER SPENDING HALF A NIGHT SEARCHING FOR PHANTOM ENGLANDERS.

UNFORTUNATELY THE TWO AIRMEN HAD LEFT AN UNINTENTIONAL MEMENTO OF THEIR OWN SHORT VISIT TO THE INN.

WHAT IS THIS, A COIN? HIMMEL, IT IS AN ENGLISH PENNY! THEY MUST HAVE BEEN HERE. TALK, INNKEEPER . . . TALK FOR YOUR VERY LIFE!

I . . . I KNOW NOTHING. NO ONE HAS BEEN HERE THIS EVENING. YOU ARE THE FIRST VISITORS I HAVE HAD.

THE GENERAL WAS IN NO MOOD TO ARGUE. HE GRABBED THE INNKEEPER'S SON.

SO YOU KNOW NOTHING? VERY WELL. YOU HAVE TEN SECONDS TO TELL ME ALL YOU KNOW NOTHING ABOUT, OR ELSE . . .

NO, NO, SPARE HIM, I BEG OF YOU. I WILL TELL YOU . . .

A FEW MINUTES LATER THE GERMANS WERE ON THE MOVE AGAIN...AND THE INN-
KEEPER WAS UNDER ARREST.

TIME TO PAY THE GOOD COUNT A VISIT, I THINK. THAT PEASANT OAF CAN BE SENT TO WORK AT THE OILFIELDS. AND COMMANDEER HIS INN — NO POINT IN HIS STOCKS GOING TO WASTE.

FATHER, FATHER...DON'T LEAVE ME!

TWENTY MINUTES LATER THE OMINOUS RUMBLE OF ENGINES IN LOW GEAR ON THE
ROAD TO THE CASTLE ALERTED HOWARD AND JOHN, BUT...

JERRIES! LET'S GET OUT OF HERE.

BLAST IT, THE DOOR'S LOCKED. THE COUNT WASN'T GOING TO TAKE ANY CHANCES WITH US. WE'LL BE OK, THOUGH. BRADU SAID HE WOULDN'T SAY ANYTHING.

DOWN BELOW, VON STACH WAS NOT WASTING ANY TIME.

WHERE IS YOUR SON, COUNT?

HE IS NOT HERE — HE IS OUT AT THE MOMENT...

THE GENERAL CAME BLUNTLY TO THE POINT.

I HAVE POSITIVE PROOF THAT YOUR SON HELPED TWO ENEMY AIRMEN TONIGHT. YOU ARE AWARE, OF COURSE, THAT WHEN WE CATCH HIM HE WILL BE SHOT?

YOU PLACE ME IN A PREDICAMENT, GENERAL. PERHAPS IF WE CAN COME TO AN AGREEMENT OVER THE FATE OF MY SON, I MIGHT BE ABLE TO TELL YOU WHERE TO FIND THE AIRMEN.

IT WAS AN INTERESTING PROPOSITION. VON STACH THOUGHT FOR A MOMENT, THEN —

VERY WELL, COUNT. IF YOU TELL ME WHERE TO FIND THE BRITISH SCHWEIN I WILL FORGET ANYTHING I HEARD ABOUT YOUR SON.

THAT IS GOOD ENOUGH. ZABA WILL SHOW YOUR MEN WHERE THEY ARE.

A COUPLE OF MINUTES LATER —

THERE THEY ARE — GRAB THEM!

GOOD GRIEF, THE COUNT MUST HAVE TOLD THEM WHERE WE WERE.

AND I THOUGHT WE WERE SAFE!

SEVERAL MILES AWAY A SIMILAR SCENE WAS BEING ENACTED AT A REMOTE FARM-HOUSE, AS SOME OF VON STACH'S MEN ON PATROL DISCOVERED BRADU AND HIS COMPANIONS.

GERMANS!

TERRORISTS WITH A RADIO — SEIZE THEM!

THERE WAS A BRIEF, BUT FIERCE BATTLE. BRADU'S TWO HELPERS FELL DEAD, AND HE HIMSELF WAS KNOCKED UNCONSCIOUS.

YOU'LL NEVER TAKE ME ALIVE...UUURGH!

THAT WAS COUNT REMPAVI'S SON. LET'S HOPE HE'S STILL ALIVE. THE GENERAL WILL BE VERY INTERESTED IF HE IS.

BACK AT THE CASTLE VON STACH WAS
READY TO LEAVE WITH THE TWO AIRMEN.

THE PRISONER WAS BRADU.

YOU
ACTED WISELY,
COUNT...

HERR GENERAL,
A PATROL IS COMING...
WITH A PRISONER.

WE FOUND
HIM AT A FARM,
OPERATING A
RADIO.

THEN HE
HAS OPERATED IT
FOR THE LAST TIME —
HE WILL BE
SHOT.

THE COUNT COULD SCARCELY BELIEVE
VON STACH COULD BE SO TREACHEROUS.

YOU PROMISED
TO LEAVE MY SON
ALONE IF I SHOWED YOU
WHERE THE BRITISH WERE
HIDING. YOU CANNOT
EXECUTE HIM.

HE WAS
FOUND OPERATING
AN ILLEGAL TRANSMITTER
AND HE RESISTED ARREST.
THE PENALTY FOR
EITHER IS DEATH.

VON STACH IGNORED ALL FURTHER PLEAS AND THE GERMANS DROVE OFF WITH THEIR PRISONERS. THE COUNT STOOD IN ANGUISH AT THE GATE. AS IF TO UNDERLINE HIS FEELINGS THE MUTTER AND RUMBLE OF THUNDER SOUNDED FROM THE INKY SKY.

MY SON, MY SON – THOSE BARBARIANS WILL SHOOT HIM AS SURELY AS NIGHT FOLLOWS DAY. ZABA, WHY IS THIS HAPPENING?

IT IS DESTINY, MASTER, AND I FEEL IT IS NOT OVER YET. PERHAPS THIS STORM IS AN OMEN...

DOWN THE MOUNTAIN THE STORM WAS ALREADY BEGINNING. THE THREE CAPTIVES SAT GLUMLY IN THE BACK OF A TRUCK.

PLEASE DON'T BLAME MY FATHER, IT WAS ALL MY FAULT. I'M SORRY I GOT YOU INTO THIS.

IF ANYONE'S TO BLAME, IT'S US TWO FOR THAT STUPID JOY-RIDE TO TAKE A CLOSE LOOK AT TRANSYLVANIA.

THE COLUMN REACHED THE BRIDGE AT THE BOTTOM OF THE ROAD AT THE SAME TIME AS THE STORM REACHED ITS HEIGHT, AND...

MEIN GOTT, THE BRIDGE HAS BEEN STRUCK BY LIGHTNING. STOP, DRIVER!

LOOK OUT!

THE TRUCK DRIVER, BLINDED BY THE FLASH, STAMPED ON THE ACCELERATOR INSTEAD OF THE BRAKES IN HIS PANIC.

NEIN... AAAGH!

THEY'RE GOING OVER... AND THEY'RE TAKING THE BRIDGE WITH THEM!

WE'RE CUT OFF. THAT BRIDGE IS THE ONLY ROAD TO TOWN.

THE GENERAL RADIOED FOR AN ENGINEER UNIT FROM BASE, AND AN HOUR LATER THEY GAVE THEIR VERDICT.

WE WILL HAVE TO BUILD A COMPLETELY NEW BRIDGE, HERR GENERAL. IT WILL TAKE AT LEAST A DAY.

VERY WELL. WE WILL WAIT AT THE CASTLE. RADIO ME AS SOON AS IT IS CLEAR.

THEY ARRIVED BACK AT THE CASTLE.

IT LOOKS AS IF WE SHALL BE YOUR GUESTS FOR LONGER THAN WE EXPECTED, COUNT.

THEN BE UNDER NO ILLUSION THAT YOU ARE WELCOME HERE. I WILL HAVE NOTHING MORE TO DO WITH YOU. ZABA WILL ATTEND TO YOUR NEEDS.

THE PRISONERS WERE THROWN INTO A FORBIDDING DUNGEON.

NOT AS COSY AS THE BEDROOM WE FIRST HAD. I SUPPOSE THERE AREN'T ANY SECRET PASSAGES OR ANYTHING, BRADU. I THOUGHT ALL OLD CASTLES WERE SUPPOSED TO HAVE THEM.

IF THERE ARE ANY, I HAVE NEVER FOUND THEM. THERE'S NO HOPE OF ESCAPING FROM HERE.

MEANWHILE ONE OF THE GERMANS HAD DISCOVERED JOHN'S ABANDONED HORROR COMICS AND WAS SHOWING THEM AROUND.

WHAT HAVE YOU GOT THERE, JOHAN?

AMERIKANER COMICS DROPPED BY ONE OF THE ENGLANDERS. ALL ABOUT VAMPIRES AND WEREWOLVES IN TRANSYLVANIA, NO LESS. HAVE A LOOK.

THE GERMANS THOUGHT THE COMICS HIGHLY AMUSING. ONE OF THEM EVEN OPENED THE PEEPHOLE AND BRANDISHED THEM. JOHN WAS FURIOUS.

HEY, THOSE ARE MINE!

JA, ENGLANDER? I HAVEN'T LAUGHED SO MUCH FOR AGES. TRANSYL-VANIA IS CRAWLING WITH BLOOD-SUCKING MONSTERS, HEIN? PERHAPS THEY WILL EVEN RESCUE YOU, JA?

MEANWHILE STRANGE THINGS WERE OCCURRING IN THE COUNT'S DRAWING ROOM. THE COUNT AND ZABA WERE ENGAGED IN SOMETHING FURTIVE...

IT IS ALL CLEAR, MASTER.

GOOD... THERE, THE PASSAGE IS OPEN. LOCK THE DOOR AND FOLLOW ME, ZABA.

THE SECRET PASSAGE LED TO A HIDDEN UNDERGROUND CRYPT.

IT IS THE FAMILY CUSTOM TO SHOW THE ELDEST SON THE SECRET WAYS ONLY AFTER HIS FATHER DIES, AS YOU SHOWED THEM TO ME, ZABA — BUT WE MUST BREAK THE TRADITION. THE BARBARIANS SHALL NOT SHOOT BRADU NOW THAT FATE HAS RETURNED HIM TO US. BRING HIM HERE, AND THE AIRMEN TOO.

AT ONCE, MASTER.

THE FIRST THE PRISONERS KNEW OF ZABA'S ARRIVAL WAS WHEN THE WALL BEHIND HOWARD SUDDENLY WASN'T THERE.

YAAH!

IT'S SLIDING BACK!

EQUALLY SUDDENLY THE HUNCHBACK APPEARED, TO EVERYONE'S AMAZEMENT.

ZABA!

BE SILENT, YOUNG MASTER. FOLLOW ME, ALL OF YOU.

WITHOUT FURTHER DELAY THEY FOLLOWED HIM BACK TO THE CRYPT. THE COUNT WAS WAITING.

FATHER, WHAT IS THIS PLACE? WHY HAVE YOU NEVER TOLD ME ABOUT IT?

THESE ARE THE TOMBS OF YOUR ANCESTORS, MY SON. THE EMPTY ONE WILL BE MINE. NORMALLY YOU WOULD ONLY HAVE BEEN TOLD OF THIS PLACE AFTER I HAD BEEN LAID TO REST, BUT I COULD HARDLY WAIT FOR THE NAZIS TO TAKE YOU AWAY AGAIN.

THE COUNT EXPLAINED EVERYTHING TO A PUZZLED HOWARD AND A GOGGLING JOHN.

YOU MEAN THE WHOLE PLACE IS RIDDLED WITH SECRET PASSAGES?

YES, BUT IT SOLVES NOTHING. THE BRIDGE IS DOWN, SO YOU ARE STRANDED AS WELL. IF YOU GOT AWAY ON FOOT THE GERMANS WOULD MISS YOU SOON – IF YOU HIDE HERE THEY WOULD SOON FIND YOU. WHAT IS TO BE DONE?

I KNOW!

THEY ALL LOOKED HOPEFULLY AT JOHN.

WE NEED TO DIVERT THE JERRIES TO GIVE US TIME TO GET AWAY. SOME OF THEM ARE LAUGHING AT MY COMICS, BUT THEY WOULDN'T LAUGH SO MUCH IF THE VAMPIRE LEGENDS TURNED OUT TO BE TRUE, WOULD THEY? AND THESE PASSAGES COULD BE USEFUL IN PERSUADING THEM.

KEEP TALKING, MY FRIEND, I'M GETTING INTERESTED.

JOHN EXPLAINED HIS PLAN, AND BRADU ADDED A FEW EMBELLISHMENTS. THE FIRST STEP MEANT RETURNING TO THE DUNGEON.

WE MUSTN'T ALERT THE GERMANS BY ESCAPING TOO SOON. IF WE STAY HERE, WE SHALL HAVE MORE TIME TO PREPARE. YOU KNOW WHERE TO FIND THE PEOPLE I TOLD YOU ABOUT, ZABA?

YES, YOUNG MASTER. REST EASY, ALL WILL BE ARRANGED.

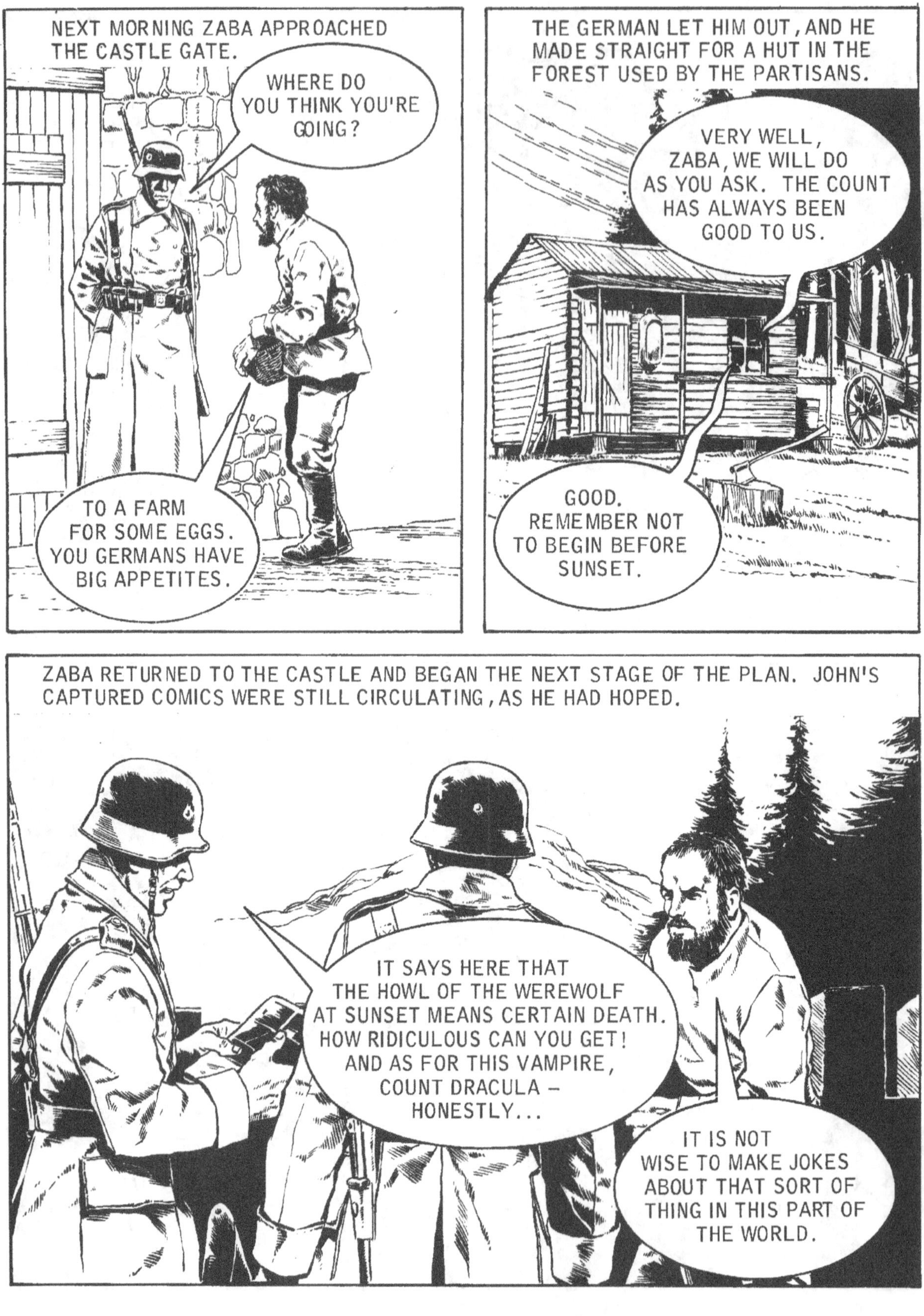

NEXT MORNING ZABA APPROACHED THE CASTLE GATE.

WHERE DO YOU THINK YOU'RE GOING?

TO A FARM FOR SOME EGGS. YOU GERMANS HAVE BIG APPETITES.

THE GERMAN LET HIM OUT, AND HE MADE STRAIGHT FOR A HUT IN THE FOREST USED BY THE PARTISANS.

VERY WELL, ZABA, WE WILL DO AS YOU ASK. THE COUNT HAS ALWAYS BEEN GOOD TO US.

GOOD. REMEMBER NOT TO BEGIN BEFORE SUNSET.

ZABA RETURNED TO THE CASTLE AND BEGAN THE NEXT STAGE OF THE PLAN. JOHN'S CAPTURED COMICS WERE STILL CIRCULATING, AS HE HAD HOPED.

IT SAYS HERE THAT THE HOWL OF THE WEREWOLF AT SUNSET MEANS CERTAIN DEATH. HOW RIDICULOUS CAN YOU GET! AND AS FOR THIS VAMPIRE, COUNT DRACULA — HONESTLY...

IT IS NOT WISE TO MAKE JOKES ABOUT THAT SORT OF THING IN THIS PART OF THE WORLD.

THE GERMANS STOPPED LAUGHING ABRUPTLY. THEY HAD NOT HEARD THE SINISTER
HUNCHBACK'S SILENT FOOT-FALLS.

ARE YOU TRYING TO SAY THERE'S SOME TRUTH IN THIS GARBAGE?

TRUTH IS WHAT YOU BELIEVE, AND PEOPLE BELIEVE STRANGE THINGS. THERE ARE EVEN LEGENDS ABOUT THIS CASTLE. IN DAY-LIGHT YOU MIGHT LAUGH THEM OFF, BUT WHEN THE MOON RIDES HIGH OVER THE MOUNTAINS, WELL...

ZABA SHRUGGED AND SIGHED EXPRESSIVELY, THEN LIMPED OFF, WHISTLING TO
HIMSELF. THE TWO GERMANS DIDN'T SEEM QUITE AS CHEERFUL AS THEY HAD BEEN...

DO YOU THINK THERE MIGHT BE SOMETHING IN WHAT THE OLD FOOL SAYS?

OLD HE MAY BE, FOOL HE IS NOT. MAYBE IT'S JUST MY IMAGINATION, BUT THIS CASTLE CAN BE PRETTY CREEPY...

AS ZABA WORKED HIS WAY ROUND THE CASTLE HE MET MANY MORE GERMANS, AND GRADUALLY THE WORD SPREAD. IT DID NOT TAKE LONG FOR VON STACH TO NOTICE SOMETHING WRONG.

WHAT ARE YOU HUDDLED THERE LIKE FRIGHTENED CHILDREN FOR? YOU, FELDWEBEL, WHAT IS HAPPENING?

IT SEEMS THE COUNT'S HUNCHBACK HAS BEEN SPREADING TALES OF VAMPIRES AND WEREWOLVES, HERR GENERAL. SOME OF THEM DON'T TOTALLY DISBELIEVE THEM. RIDICULOUS, OF COURSE, BUT...

VON STACH COULD HARDLY BELIEVE IT.

YOU MEAN SOME OF THESE CLOWNS ACTUALLY BELIEVE THESE FAIRY TALES? THEY ARE BIGGER IDIOTS THAN I THOUGHT. I SHALL TELL THE COUNT TO KEEP HIS SERVANT QUIET IN FUTURE. AND YOU, GIVE THESE MEN SOME WORK TO KEEP THEM BUSY.

THE GENERAL STRODE INTO THE GREAT HALL ANGRILY. BUT STILL THE SOLDIERS WONDERED —

THE COUNT NEVER SHOWS HIMSELF IN DAYLIGHT, YOU KNOW...

SO THAT MAKES HIM A VAMPIRE, DOES IT? RIGHT, YOU LOT, YOU HEARD THE GENERAL. IT'S TIME TO KEEP YOUR MINDS OCCUPIED, AND YOU CAN START BY WASHING DOWN THE TRUCKS!

VON STACH FOUND THE COUNT BROODING QUIETLY IN A DARK CORNER.

SO THERE YOU ARE! I DEMAND YOU ORDER YOUR SERVANT TO STOP UPSETTING MY MEN WITH WILD TALES OF MONSTERS AND THE LIKE!

ZABA HAS FRIGHTENED YOUR BRAVE GERMAN SOLDIERS WITH HIS FAIRY STORIES? I CAN HARDLY BELIEVE THAT. PERHAPS YOU BELIEVE IN THEM ALSO?

THE GENERAL NEARLY EXPLODED.

AS IF I WOULD BELIEVE SUCH RUBBISH! JUST BE CAREFUL, COUNT. WE'LL BE HERE FOR ANOTHER NIGHT, AND IF ANYTHING HAPPENS I'LL TAKE DRASTIC REPRISALS. YOU HAVE BEEN WARNED!

THANK YOU, GENERAL. NOW PLEASE LEAVE ME ALONE. YOUR PRESENCE OFFENDS ME, AS YOU NO DOUBT KNOW.

SO ZABA SAID NO MORE — NOT THAT IT MADE ANY DIFFERENCE. THE OCCUPYING GERMANS HAD HAD THE SEED OF DOUBT SOWN, AND AS NIGHT FELL A CHILLING HOWL CAME FROM THE FOREST.

THE TERRIBLE SOUND SENT A SHIVER OF FEAR THROUGH EVERYONE THAT HEARD IT, BUT FOR THE SENTRY AT THE GATE IT WAS TERRIFYING.

THERE IT IS AGAIN. IT CAN'T BE A WOLF, I'VE NEVER HEARD ONE HOWL LIKE THAT...

A RUSTLE BEHIND HIM MADE THE SENTRY WHIRL ROUND, TO COME FACE TO FACE WITH...

WHO IS... NEIN... AAAGH!

THE SCREAMS BROUGHT OUT THE GERMANS, BUT THEY WERE TOO LATE — THE MAN WAS VERY, VERY DEAD.

THIS IS HOW WE FOUND HIM, HERR GENERAL. ATTACKED BY SOME STRANGE BEAST. THERE ARE TWO PUNCTURE-MARKS IN HIS THROAT!

ANOTHER SCREAM, HERR GENERAL, FROM INSIDE THE CASTLE!

INSIDE THE CASTLE THEY FOUND ANOTHER BODY.

HE HAS BEEN KILLED THE SAME WAY.

THE SAME WAY... THE SAME MARKS! IT COULD ONLY HAVE BEEN ONE THING — A VAMPIRE...

SILENCE!

THE GERMAN TROOPS WERE BADLY SHAKEN. RAPIDLY VON STACH TOOK FIRM COMMAND.

ONCE AND FOR ALL, THERE'S NOTHING SUPERNATURAL ABOUT THIS, AND I'LL PROVE IT. BRING THE COUNT AND HIS SERVANT TO THE GREAT HALL. THEY'RE BEHIND THIS, I'M CERTAIN.

JAWOHL, HERR GENERAL, AT ONCE!

BUT AFTER TWENTY MINUTES OF SEARCHING NOTHING COULD BE FOUND OF THE COUNT AND ZABA.

WE HAVE SEARCHED EVERY ROOM IN THE CASTLE, HERR GENERAL, BUT THERE'S NO SIGN OF THEM.

THIS IS INTOLERABLE! THEY MUST BE SOMEWHERE. GET THE REST OF THE MEN TO HELP — I WANT THOSE TWO FOUND!

DOWN IN THE DUNGEON THE TIME HAD COME FOR THE PRISONERS TO DISAPPEAR.

IT IS TIME FOR YOU TO PLAY YOUR PART. COME...

BEFORE SLIDING BACK THE STONE ZABA RELEASED THREE CAGED BATS INTO THE CELL.

YOU GOT SOME BATS THEN?

AS YOU AIRMEN ARE PAINFULLY AWARE, THE BELL TOWER HOUSES THOUSANDS. THERE THEY GO...

THEY SLID THE STONE BACK AND MADE THEIR WAY TO THE CRYPT WHERE THE COUNT WAS WAITING.

HOW'S IT GOING?

VERY WELL, SO FAR. BRADU'S COMPANIONS ARE USING MEGAPHONES IN THE FOREST TO GIVE US SUITABLE HOWLS, AND THIS SPIKED GAUNTLET FROM MY ANCESTOR'S ARMOUR HAS ALREADY DEALT WITH TWO GERMANS. BUT VON STACH IS NOT BEING FOOLED LIKE HIS MEN, SO WE MUST MOVE QUICKLY.

MEANWHILE THE ESCAPE HAD BEEN DISCOVERED.

I SWEAR TO YOU, HERR GENERAL, THREE PRISONERS WERE THERE FIVE MINUTES AGO. BUT NOW THERE ARE THREE BATS! THERE IS NO WAY OUT APART FROM THE DOOR. WHAT DOES IT MEAN?

IT MEANS WE'VE BEEN TRICKED — MEN DO NOT TURN INTO BATS! I WANT THIS CASTLE COMBED FROM TOP TO BOTTOM!

THE FRANTIC SEARCH BEGAN, BUT THE CASTLE'S HIDDEN WAYS GAVE THE FUGITIVES ALL THE ADVANTAGES.

UGH!

FOR ZABA, WEAPONS WERE UNNECESSARY. HIS IMMENSELY POWERFUL ARMS WERE LIKE A VICE.

DIE, BARBARIAN!

NEIN... URRGH!

THE UNEASINESS OF THE TROOPS SOON TURNED INTO NEAR-PANIC. ARMED GUERILLAS THEY COULD FIGHT WITH PROFESSIONAL SKILL, BUT THIS WAS DIFFERENT.

SEVEN DEAD, CUT DOWN IN APPARENTLY EMPTY ROOMS AND CORRIDORS. WHAT ARE WE TRYING TO FIGHT...MEN OR PHANTOMS?

MEN, YOU DOGS, MEN! LOOK AT YOU – GERMANY'S FINEST TROOPS ACTING LIKE A RABBLE OF FRIGHTENED SCHOOLGIRLS JUST BECAUSE OF SOME AMERIKANER COMICS AND A HUNCHBACK WITH A WAGGING TONGUE!

SUDDENLY A STIFLED CRY MADE THE GERMANS TURN, JUST IN TIME TO SEE THE COUNT CLAIM ANOTHER VICTIM.

LOOK, LOOK, THERE! THE COUNT AND ONE OF OUR MEN.

BARBARIANS! LEAVE THIS PLACE NOW, OR NONE OF YOU WILL EVER SEE YOUR HOMES AGAIN!

SHOOT HIM DOWN!

LIVID, THE GENERAL PULLED OUT HIS PISTOL AND OPENED FIRE. THE COUNT TURNED AND RAN.

SEE — SINCE WHEN HAVE PHANTOMS SOUGHT COVER FROM BULLETS? AFTER HIM.

HE IS TRAPPED, HERR GENERAL. THAT PASSAGEWAY IS A DEAD END . . . IN MORE WAYS THAN ONE, AS FAR AS THE COUNT IS CONCERNED.

SCENTING VICTORY, VON STACH LED HIS MEN TO THE PASSAGE, BUT...

WHERE...
WHERE HAS HE
GONE? HE'S
VANISHED.

HE'S VANISHED
BECAUSE HE ISN'T
HUMAN. NOTHING IN
THIS PLACE IS HUMAN.
HE WARNED US WHAT
WOULD HAPPEN IF
WE STAYED...

AS THE GERMANS MILLED AROUND IN PANIC, OTHER EYES WATCHED THEM FROM THE
HIGH BELL TOWER. HOWARD AND JOHN HAD TAKEN THEIR POSITION FOR THE FINAL
PHASE OF THE OPERATION.

THE COUNT'S
PERFORMANCE HAS
REALLY GOT THEM WORRIED.
ZABA MUST HAVE HAD THE
SECRET PASSAGE OPEN
AND WAITING.

I THINK IT'S
TIME FOR THE FINALE.
LET'S START THE BELL
RINGING. ZABA SAID IT
HADN'T BEEN RUNG FOR
YEARS, SO THE BATS
SHOULD GET QUITE
A SHOCK.

SECONDS LATER THE GREAT BELL BEGAN TO TOLL.

THE BELL! IT'S OUR FINAL WARNING!

RUBBISH! STAND FIRM!

SUDDENLY THE AIR WAS THICK WITH BATS AS THE ENTIRE COLONY STREAMED FROM THE BELL TOWER, DRIVEN OUT BY THE VIBRATIONS. IT WAS THE LAST STRAW FOR THE FRIGHTENED TROOPS.

BATS, BATS! RUN, RUN FOR YOUR LIVES! GET INTO THE TRUCKS!

COWARDLY SCUM! I ORDER YOU TO STOP!

NOTHING ON EARTH COULD HAVE HALTED THE PANIC NOW, LEAST OF ALL MAJOR POEST, WHO DIED IN A VALIANT BUT FUTILE ATTEMPT.

GET OUT OF THE WAY OR WE RUN YOU OVER!

NEIN! YOU WILL OBEY GENERAL VON STACH, OR I SHOOT... AAAGH!

ON THE EDGE OF THE FOREST THE GUERILLAS WHO HAD SUPPLIED THE HOWLS WATCHED THE PANIC-STRICKEN ROUT.

HERE THEY COME, WHITE WITH TERROR. SERVES THEM RIGHT FOR BELIEVING STUPID OLD LEGENDS. TIME TO LAY OUT THE WELCOMING MAT, BOYS.

THE WELCOMING MAT CONSISTED OF SEVERAL BARRELS OF OIL SPREAD ONTO THE ROAD SURFACE.

WHAT ARE THEY DOING? BLITZEN, THEY'RE COVERING THE ROAD WITH OIL! I'LL NEVER STOP IN TIME...

NONE OF THE TRUCKS COULD AVOID THE DEADLY SURFACE. ONE AFTER ANOTHER THEY SLITHERED OFF THE MOUNTAIN ROAD — INTO OBLIVION.

AAAAGH!

HOW DO YOU LIKE OUR GOOD RUMANIAN OIL, NAZIS? I BET YOU NEVER THOUGHT OF USING IT IN SUCH A USEFUL WAY!

VON STACH WATCHED THE DESTRUCTION WITH A GRIM FURY.

OBVIOUSLY THIS WAS ALL PLANNED FROM THE BEGINNING. VERY WELL, COUNT REMPAVI. FIRST I WILL KILL YOU AND YOUR SON AND THEN I'LL HAVE THIS CASTLE WIPED OFF THE FACE OF THE EARTH!

JUST THE SORT OF NOBLE SENTIMENT I'D EXPECT FROM YOU, GENERAL!

HE SPUN ROUND AT THE SOUND OF THE COUNT'S VOICE.

SO YOU'VE COME TO SAVE ME THE TROUBLE OF FLUSHING YOU OUT.

ANYTHING TO OBLIGE...BUT YOU WILL HAVE TO CATCH ME FIRST!

VON STACH OPENED FIRE AS THE COUNT DODGED INTO A DOORWAY. EVEN AS THE GENERAL GAVE CHASE, THE OTHERS APPEARED.

THANKS TO YOU WE HAVE SCORED A GREAT VICTORY OVER THE HUNS. NOW WE ONLY HAVE TO DEAL WITH THE GENERAL ...GRIEF, HE'S AFTER MY FATHER!

YOU WON'T ESCAPE THIS TIME, COUNT!

AS THEY GAVE CHASE VON STACH WAS ALREADY CATCHING UP WITH HIS QUARRY.

HIDDEN PASSAGES! NOW ALL YOUR PARTY TRICKS BECOME CLEAR!

CATCH ME THEN, GENERAL, IF IT'S SO EASY...

THE CHASE ENDED IN THE CRYPT.

THE S.S. GENERAL SQUEEZED THE TRIGGER SEVERAL TIMES.

MY PLEASURE, COUNT.

NOW I HAVE YOU. BREATHE YOUR LAST, COUNT — I WILL SHOW YOU NO MERCY.

THEN KILL ME, VON STACH... IF YOU DARE!

THE OTHERS HAD JUST REACHED THE ENTRANCE TO THE PASSAGE WHEN THE SHOTS RANG OUT.

TOO LATE. VON STACH GOT TO HIM FIRST.

FATHER, FATHER! THE THINGS I CALLED YOU, AND YET YOU FOUGHT MORE BRAVELY THAN ANY OF US. LET ME GET HOLD OF THAT GENERAL — I'LL TEAR HIM APART WITH MY BARE HANDS!

AS THE TWO AIRMEN TRIED TO STOP BRADU BLUNDERING INTO A POSSIBLE AMBUSH, A BLOOD-CURDLING SCREAM SOUNDED FROM DEEP IN THE PASSAGE.

HANG ON, THAT JERRY MIGHT BE WAITING FOR YOU... YE GODS, WHAT WAS THAT?

THAT WAS A SCREAM, OLD SON, THE MOST HORRIBLE SCREAM I'VE EVER HEARD. WHAT THE DEVIL'S HAPPENING IN THERE?

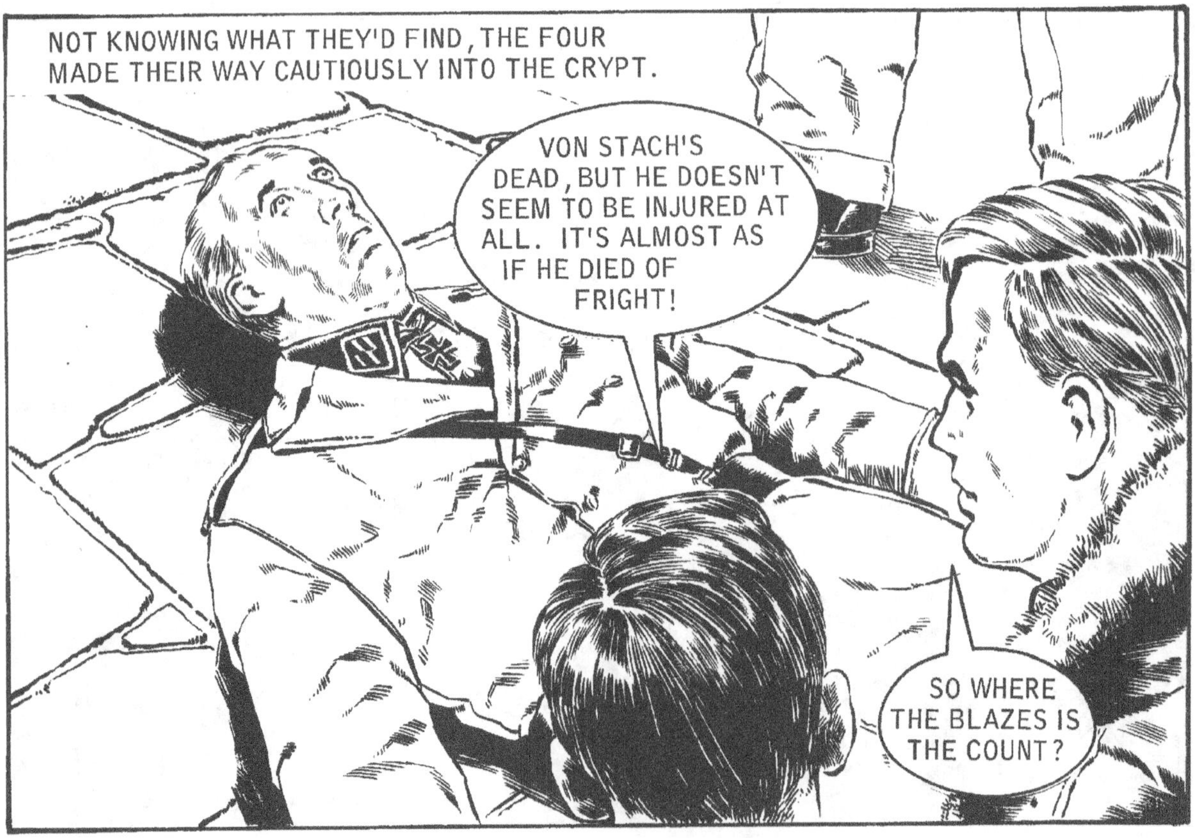

NOT KNOWING WHAT THEY'D FIND, THE FOUR MADE THEIR WAY CAUTIOUSLY INTO THE CRYPT.

VON STACH'S DEAD, BUT HE DOESN'T SEEM TO BE INJURED AT ALL. IT'S ALMOST AS IF HE DIED OF FRIGHT!

SO WHERE THE BLAZES IS THE COUNT?

AS HOWARD CHECKED VON STACH'S GUN, JOHN SUDDENLY NOTICED SOMETHING DIFFERENT ABOUT THE CRYPT.

HIS GUN'S BEEN FIRED SEVERAL TIMES. THE MAG'S EMPTY.

I'VE JUST REALISED SOMETHING. THAT TOMB AT THE END WAS EMPTY BEFORE, WITH THE LID LEANING BY THE SIDE. WHO PUT IT ON TOP?

WHO COULD HAVE? AND WHY?

AS ONE MAN, HOWARD, JOHN AND BRADU, STEPPED FORWARD AND HEAVED OFF THE HEAVY STONE LID. ZABA WATCHED CLOSELY, A SLIGHT SMILE ON HIS UGLY FEATURES.

PHEW, THIS THING WEIGHS A TON. WHAT ARE WE EXPECTING TO FIND INSIDE?

I THINK I KNOW THE ANSWER TO THAT ALREADY.

EVERYONE EXCEPT ZABA GASPED WHEN THEY SAW THE BODY OF THE COUNT LYING PEACEFULLY IN HIS TOMB.

MY FATHER... DEAD! BUT WHERE ARE THE BULLET WOUNDS — AND HOW DID HE GET INSIDE HERE?

PERHAPS ONLY ONE OR TWO SHOTS HIT HIM WHICH WE CAN'T SEE, AND KNOWING HE WAS DYING HE CRAWLED INTO THE TOMB THAT WAS TO BE HIS.

JOHN SNORTED.

COME OFF IT, ZABA. HOW COULD A DYING MAN GET IN HERE AND THEN PULL THAT LID OVER THE TOP? THREE OF US COULD ONLY JUST BUDGE IT! AND WHAT ABOUT VON STACH? PERHAPS HE'S GOT A BUMP ON THE HEAD THAT WE HAVEN'T NOTICED!

ZABA, YOU SEEMED TO BE EXPECTING THIS. WHAT DOES IT MEAN? WHAT HAPPENED IN HERE BEFORE MY FATHER DIED? WHAT ARE THE REAL SECRETS IN THIS CASTLE?

THE FAITHFUL OLD SERVANT SIGHED, AND THEN SMILED A LITTLE.

THERE ARE MANY SECRETS IN CASTLE REMPAVI, YOUNG MASTER. MOST OF THEM HAVE DIED WITH YOUR FATHER. HE WAS THE LAST OF THE TRADITIONAL LINE — YOU ARE DIFFERENT. PERHAPS MY EXPLANATION IS INSUFFICIENT, BUT IT WILL DO. NOW LET US THINK ABOUT THE FUTURE.

THEY DID AS THE OLD HUNCHBACK ASKED, AND LATER CAME THE PARTING OF WAYS.

FAREWELL, MY FRIENDS. I WOULD GUIDE YOU TO SAFETY MYSELF, BUT ZABA INSISTS I TAKE TO THE MOUNTAINS WITH MY MEN UNTIL THE GERMANS FORGET ABOUT THIS INCIDENT. HE IS RIGHT, I SUPPOSE.

OF COURSE HE'S RIGHT, AND HE'LL LOOK AFTER US BETTER THAN ANYONE. WE'LL NEVER FORGET YOU. MAYBE AFTER THE WAR WE CAN MEET AGAIN. I'VE STILL GOT A LOT OF QUESTIONS UNANSWERED.

ZABA LED THEM ACROSS THE COUNTRY TO THE YUGOSLAV BORDER.

THESE MEN ARE PARTISANS. THEY WILL MAKE SURE YOU REACH ITALY. I MUST RETURN TO THE CASTLE NOW. FAREWELL, ENGLISHMEN.

THEY STOOD FOR A MOMENT WATCHING AS ZABA LIMPED AWAY.

QUITE A CHARACTER. IMAGINE GOING BACK TO THAT EMPTY CASTLE.

MAYBE IT WON'T BE THAT EMPTY — NOT THAT WE'LL EVER KNOW.

A FEW WEEKS LATER THEY WERE BACK IN ITALY AND BACK ON OPS. ONE EVENING IN THE MESS —

I DON'T SUPPOSE YOU'D KNOW IF REMPAVI WAS A COMMON RUMANIAN NAME, WOULD YOU?

NO, I WOULDN'T. WHY, ANY-WAY?

JOHN HELD UP THE PIECE OF PAPER HE HAD BEEN SCRIBBLING ON.

FUNNY WHAT YOU CAN DO WHEN YOU PLAY AROUND WITH LETTERS. SAME LETTERS REARRANGED, AND SEE WHAT YOU GET — VAMPIRE!

REMPAVI
VIPAMRE
AMIVRE
PVIRE
VAMPIRE

I DON'T REALLY THINK I WANT TO KNOW, THANKS ALL THE SAME...

AND BOTH MEN VERY MUCH DOUBTED IF THEY WOULD EVER KNOW THE TRUTH OF THE COUNT REMPAVI AND HIS SINISTER CASTLE. AFTER ALL, NOBODY BELIEVES IN VAMPIRES... DO THEY?

Commando
THE END

Commando
FOR ACTION AND ADVENTURE

OPERATION
Silver Bullets

Follow the trail of bodies to Chateau Epouvantail and you're sure of a big surprise. The Nazis there are bigger than average, stronger than most. They can see the sweat drip down your face in the dark; hear your heartbeat from a mile away. And when you're close enough to see what big teeth they have, then it's too late for you, my friend...

Commando

FOR ACTION AND ADVENTURE

www.commandocomics.com

COMPLETE 63-PAGE ACTION STORY
Commando
FOR ACTION AND ADVENTURE
OPERATION
Silver Bullets

Story: KEK-W

Kek-W is a pseudonym adopted by writer Nigel Long while working for legendary sci-fi comic *2000 AD*. Kek-W has written for a variety of titles, including Rebellion's Monster Fun Halloween Spectacular Special and Judge Dredd Megazine. So far 'Operation Silver Bullets' is the only *Commando* to have been written by Kek-W, but as Nigel Long, KEK-W penned #4849 'Charge – or Die!'.

Art: Jaume Forns

Jaume Forns Bargeno was born in Barcelona in 1939. Forns had a love of comics from a young age and has been drawing since he was a child. When Forns turned 18, he was hired to work as an illustrator by Graficas Ricard on fairytale and romance comics. In 1961, Forns began work for Toray Editions, drawing the *Fulgor* collection. Later, he joined the team of Hazañaz Belicas created by Boixcar, drawing the *Ben-Hur* stories and *The Three Musketeers*. He has also worked for French and German comics. Forns has worked for DC Thomson for 20 years, on syndicated equestrian title *Wendy*, as well as *Commando*, producing artwork for over 50 issues since 2012.

Cover: Tom Foster

Born in Glasgow, Tom Foster began his British Comics career when he won the *2000 AD* portfolio competition in 2013. He soon began working regularly for *2000 AD* and *Judge Dredd Megazine.* Foster was recruited to *Commando* by editor Gordon Tait, and his first *Commando* Cover was #5251 'Faceless Heroes' in 2019. Tom continues to work on Judge Dredd and is a firm fan favourite amongst the Squaxx Dek Thargo!

LOCAL GAMEKEEPER, MIKE FOXE, AND HIS SON, CHARLIE, HEARD ADAM'S CRIES.

OI! LEAVE HIM ALONE, YOU BLIGHTER!

WELL, THIS EXPLAINS THE TRACKS WE FOUND. MUST'VE ESCAPED FROM THE ZOO.

IT...IT BIT ME! BUT MY BOOK TOOK THE WORST OF IT.

ADAM WASN'T SERIOUSLY INJURED, BUT THE PAIN AND STRESS HAD AGGRAVATED HIS ASTHMA.

142

GOOD FOR YOU, CHARLIE! I TRIED TO ENLIST, BUT MY WRETCHED ASTHMA... COUGH-COUGH!
DON'T LET IT GET YOU DOWN, ADAM. THERE'S PLENTY OF WAYS A BRIGHT BLOKE LIKE YOU CAN DO THEIR BIT.

BUT HOW, CHARLIE?
I'M A ZOOLOGIST — NOT AN ENGINEER!
13

WALKING BACK TO HIS LODGINGS NEAR THE UNIVERSITY, ADAM WAS SURPRISED TO BUMP INTO A MAN WITH A MYSTERIOUS BLACK CAR.
MISTER HANLEY?
ER, YES, AND WHO ARE YOU?
A WORD. IN THE CAR — NOW!
YESSIR!

I'M BROOKS, ARMY INTELLIGENCE. WE'VE HAD OUR EYE ON YOU FOR A WHILE NOW, HANLEY.
YOUR CREDENTIALS ARE IMPRESSIVE — YOUNGEST PROFESSOR IN BRITAIN...OUR LEADING EXPERT IN LUPINE PHYSIOLOGY.
I AM. GOODNESS, THIS IS LIKE BEING IN AN EDGAR WALLACE SPY THRILLER!

ADAM WAS WHISKED AWAY TO A SECRET LOCATION IN WHITEHALL.

THIS IS SIR WILLIAM BRIERLY, FROM THE MINISTRY.

SORRY FOR THE DRAMA, PROFESSOR, THERE'S SOMETHING TOP SECRET WE'D LIKE YOUR OPINION ON. BUT FIRST WHAT, MAY I ASK, IS... THAT?

REMARKABLE!

THIS? A DRY POWDER INHALER — FOR MY ASTHMA. THERE WAS NOTHING ON THE MARKET, SO I MADE ONE.

NOW, THIS FOOTAGE IS FROM A FRENCH RESISTANCE RECONNAISSANCE MISSION THAT WENT TRAGICALLY WRONG.

GOOD LORD! WOLVES... HUMAN WOLVES! HOW'S THAT POSSIBLE?

I WAS HOPING YOU MIGHT BE ABLE TO TELL US.

WELL, FROM WHAT WE KNOW ABOUT GENETICS, IT'S POSSIBLE THAT WOLF-LIKE ATTRIBUTES OR MUTATIONS COULD BE INTRODUCED INTO AN INDIVIDUAL.

THERE'S A GERMAN BIOLOGIST — HERMAN WEISE — I READ HIS PRE-WAR WORK ON HEREDITY, BUT FOUND IT TROUBLING.

GOOD. WE ACTUALLY SUSPECT WEISE IS BEHIND THIS. BUT WHY WOLVES, PROFESSOR?

WOLF SOLDIERS COULD BE FAST AND FEROCIOUS, OPERATE IN PACKS — HAVE NIGHT VISION, ENHANCED SENSES.

IT'S A PSYCHOLOGICAL WEAPON AS MUCH AS A PHYSICAL ONE. IMAGINE THE EFFECT ON OUR OWN SOLDIERS — OR CIVILIANS!

I'VE PUT TOGETHER A SPECIAL COMMANDO UNIT. CAPTAIN BROOKS IS OUR INTELLIGENCE LIAISON.

WE'D LIKE YOU TO HELP DEVELOP COUNTERMEASURES AGAINST THESE WOLFMEN, PROFESSOR.

WHY, SIR! I'D BE HONOURED.

WE'LL NEED A CODENAME. OPERATION: KEEP THE WOLF AT BAY, PERHAPS?

NO, TOO LONG WINDED! RABIES? MUZZLE?

HOW ABOUT OPERATION: SILVER BULLET?

PERFECT! WELCOME ABOARD, PROFESSOR.

ADAM GOT STUCK IN. THE WORK WAS CHALLENGING, BUT HELPED HIM FACE HIS OWN INSECURITIES AND PHYSICAL FRAILTIES.

WHAT'RE YOU COOKING UP IN HERE?

LIGHT SOUND
CAPSALUN ↑ SMELL
SENSE
GALTON'S WHISTLE

WAYS OF KEEPING YOU CHAPS SAFE. TRY THOSE ARM GUARDS ON FOR SIZE.

IF THAT BOOK HADN'T COME BETWEEN ME AND THAT WOLF I WOULDN'T BE HERE NOW.

IT WAS TIME TO TRY OUT SOME OF ADAM'S IDEAS.

CRIKEY! I FEEL LIKE BLOOMIN' SPARTACUS IN THIS GET-UP!

THE PROFESSOR SAYS THIS WILL GET YOU USED TO LARGE, AGGRESSIVE DOGS — TEACH YOU TO KEEP YOUR COOL.

BUT KEN BAILEY WASN'T HAPPY WITH ADAM OR HIS METHODS. HE WAS A THREAT TO THE STATUS QUO.

DON'T GET TOO PALLY WITH THAT ONE, TOTO — HE'S NOT ONE OF US. HIS CRACKPOT IDEAS WILL GET SOMEONE KILLED!

I DON'T THINK YOUR SERGEANT APPROVES OF ME.

HIS BARK'S WORSE THAN HIS BITE, IF YOU GET MY, ER, DRIFT. LET ME HAVE A QUIET WORD...

HIS IDEAS ARE SOUND, SERGEANT. HE ONLY WANTS TO HELP.

BROOKS LUMBERED ME WITH HIM, BUT IT DOESN'T MEAN I HAVE TO LIKE IT.

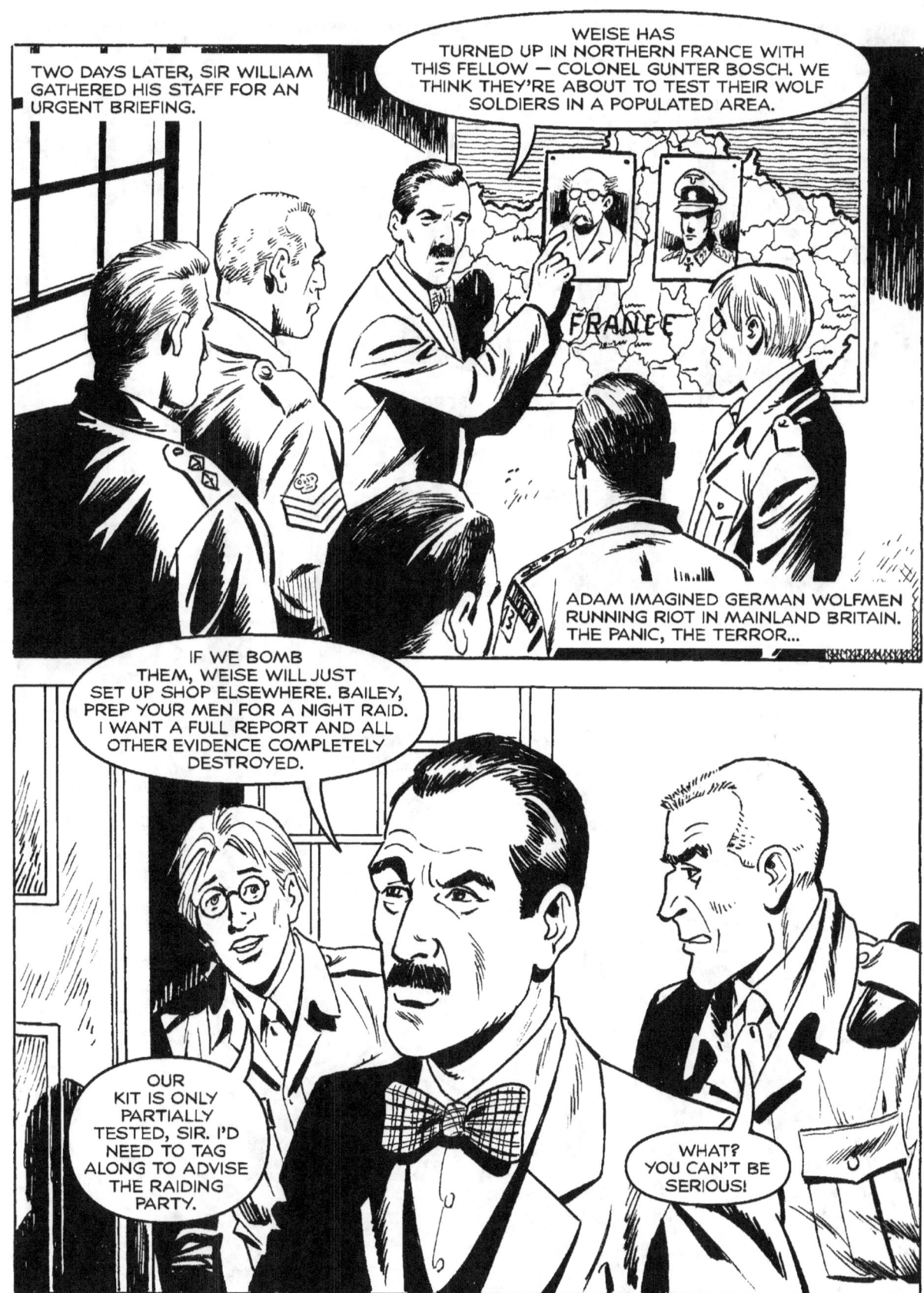

TWO DAYS LATER, SIR WILLIAM GATHERED HIS STAFF FOR AN URGENT BRIEFING.

WEISE HAS TURNED UP IN NORTHERN FRANCE WITH THIS FELLOW — COLONEL GUNTER BOSCH. WE THINK THEY'RE ABOUT TO TEST THEIR WOLF SOLDIERS IN A POPULATED AREA.

FRANCE

ADAM IMAGINED GERMAN WOLFMEN RUNNING RIOT IN MAINLAND BRITAIN. THE PANIC, THE TERROR...

IF WE BOMB THEM, WEISE WILL JUST SET UP SHOP ELSEWHERE. BAILEY, PREP YOUR MEN FOR A NIGHT RAID. I WANT A FULL REPORT AND ALL OTHER EVIDENCE COMPLETELY DESTROYED.

OUR KIT IS ONLY PARTIALLY TESTED, SIR. I'D NEED TO TAG ALONG TO ADVISE THE RAIDING PARTY.

WHAT? YOU CAN'T BE SERIOUS!

WITH RESPECT, SIR. HANLEY'S A LIABILITY. MY MEN ARE MY PRIORITY — NOT MOLLYCODDLING HIM!

NOTED, BUT OVERRULED. WE'LL NEED HIM ON HAND TO ANALYSE WHATEVER WE FIND OVER THERE.

I'LL PERSONALLY KEEP HIM OUT OF HARM'S WAY.

THANK YOU, CAPTAIN BROOKS.

LISTEN, STAFFIE, I'M SORRY IF I'VE PUT YOUR NOSE OUT OF JOINT —

THAT'S "STAFF SERGEANT" TO YOU, SUNSHINE! DO ANYTHING THAT ENDANGERS MY LADS AND I'LL PERSONALLY FEED YOU TO ONE OF THOSE OVERGROWN GERMAN SHEPHERDS — GOT IT?

Y-YES, STAFF SERGEANT.

THE BRITTANY COAST, 36 HOURS LATER.

NERVOUS, ADAM?

HE'LL BE FINE. JUST STICK TO ME LIKE GLUE, HANLEY.

NO OFFENCE TO THE PROF, BUT WON'T THESE ARM GUARDS JUST GET IN THE WAY?

YEAH, LIKE HIM. KEEP THEM ON — IN CASE WE ENCOUNTER BRAMBLES OR GET ATTACKED BY KITTENS, HA-HA.

OVERHEARING THE INSULT STUNG. ANOTHER WEEK AND ADAM WOULD HAVE REFINED HIS PROTOTYPES — MADE THEM LIGHTER, LESS CUMBERSOME.

BROOKS TOOK A SILENT DOG-WHISTLE FROM HIS POCKET AND BLEW IT. THE WOLFMEN STOPPED, AS IF THEY HAD BEEN CONDITIONED TO RESPOND.

BROOKS? W-WHAT ARE YOU —

YOU'RE A TRAITOR — A DOUBLE-AGENT!

BRITAIN CAN'T WIN THIS WAR, HANLEY. ONLY A FOOL WOULD PICK THE LOSING SIDE.

MY MISSION WAS TO BRING YOU HERE TO ASSIST DOCTOR WEISE — NOT STOP HIM.

NOW YOU CAN STUDY HIS WOLFSOLDATEN FIRST-HAND!

BROOKS SENT THE WOLFMEN BACK DOWN THE CLIFF PATH WITH A SINGLE COMMAND IN GERMAN —

TOTEN!

"KILL!"

YOU TREACHEROUS, COLD-HEARTED MONSTER!
CONSIDER THIS AN EXPERIMENT AND THIRTEEN COMMANDO THE TEST SUBJECTS. THEY'RE EXPENDABLE...

"...MERE WOLF FODDER!"
HOLD UP! SOMEONE'S COMING – PROBABLY BROOKS AND HIS FRENCH CONTACTS.
HANG ON. CAN I HEAR... DOGS?

THEY'RE EVERYWHERE!
HOLD YOUR GROUND! FIRE AT WILL!

AAGH!
THESE THINGS... T-THEY'RE REAL!

ESCAPE WAS IMPOSSIBLE.

EVEN STAFFIE WAS IN TROUBLE.
IT — IT'S STILL COMING!

DEAD! TOOK A WHOLE MAGAZINE TO PUT IT DOWN!
TOLD YOU WE NEEDED SOMETHING WITH MORE CLOUT — LIKE THIS!

I'VE NEVER SEEN THE LIKE... GUESS WE'VE GOT OUR REPORT.
CAN YOU IMAGINE AN ARMY OF THOSE THINGS?

IT'S UP TO US TO MAKE SURE THAT DOESN'T HAPPEN.
13

THE SON OF A GAMEKEEPER, CHARLIE USED HIS TRACKING SKILLS TO PICK UP ADAM'S TRAIL.

SOMETHING'S OFF HERE. WHY'S ADAM WALKING IN FRONT OF CAPTAIN BROOKS?

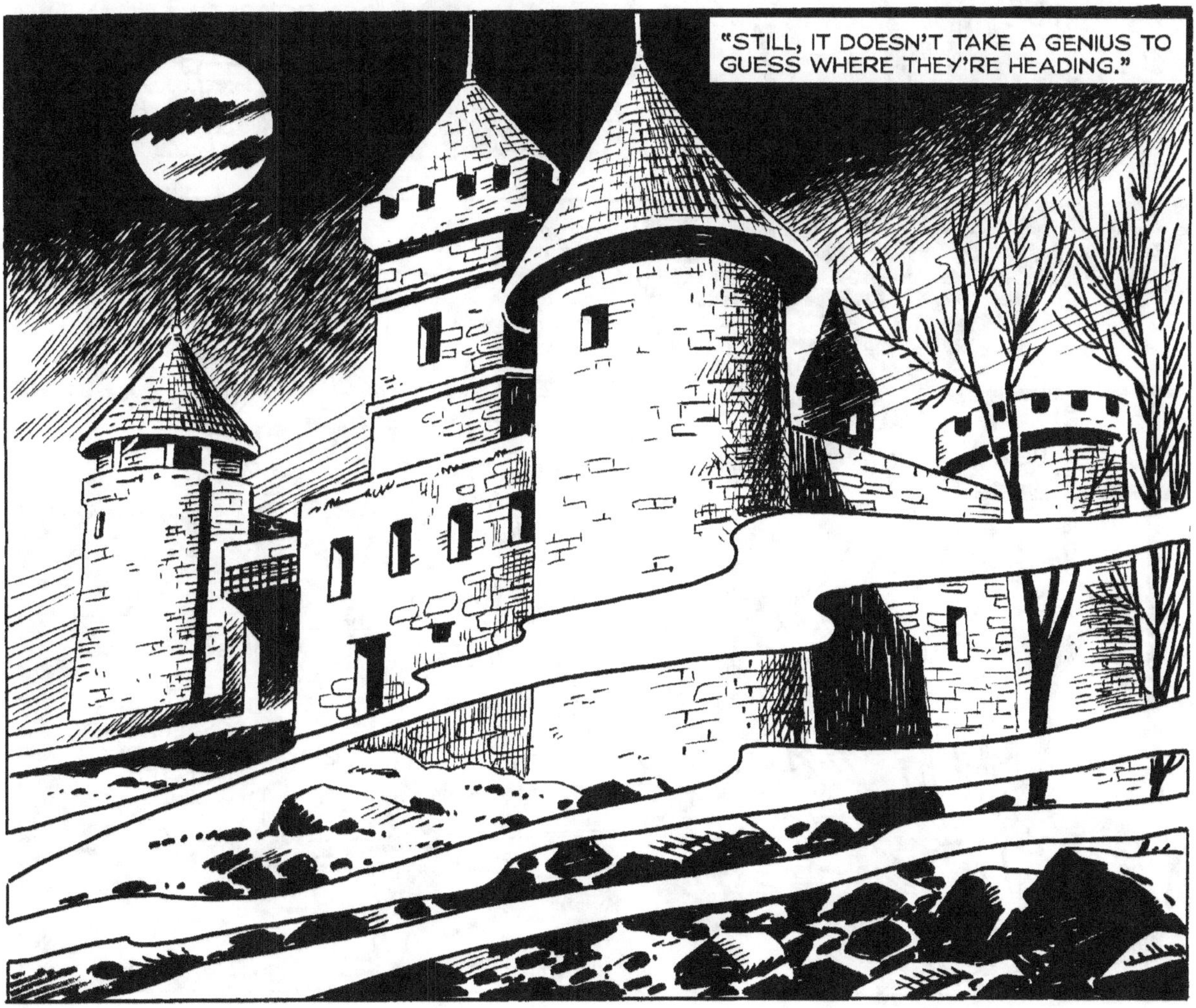

"STILL, IT DOESN'T TAKE A GENIUS TO GUESS WHERE THEY'RE HEADING."

INSIDE CHATEAU EPOUVANTAIL.

I'VE DELIVERED HANLEY TO YOU, AS AGREED, COLONEL BOSCH. WHEN DO I GET MY PAYMENT?

IS THIS QUICK ENOUGH?

UGH!

MEN LIKE HIM HAVE NO LOYALTY. THEY CANNOT BE TRUSTED.

YOU WILL ASSIST DOCTOR WEISE IN DEVELOPING A NEW GENERATION OF WOLFSOLDATEN. SOLDIERS THAT NEVER TIRE, THAT HUNT THEIR ENEMY LIKE PREY...

...AND WHICH ARE COMPLETELY OBEDIENT!

"OUR EARLY WOLF HYBRIDS WERE SAVAGE, FERAL — THE PERFECT TERROR WEAPON!"

"IDEAL FOR PACIFYING CIVILIANS AND CRUSHING RESISTANCE."

"BUT THEY WERE DIFFICULT TO CONTROL, WOULD TURN ON THEIR HANDLERS."

YOU AND I WILL CREATE PACKS OF HUMAN WOLVES — SAVAGE, UNSTOPPABLE AND LOYAL TO THE FATHERLAND!

YOU'RE MAD! GO AHEAD AND SHOOT — I WON'T HELP YOU MAKE MORE OF THESE ABOMINATIONS!

YOU TALK TOUGH, BUT I'VE SEEN YOUR FILE. YOU'RE WEAK AND NEUROTIC — A TYPICAL ENGLISH ACADEMIC.

WE'LL SOON BREAK YOUR SPIRIT! COLONEL, SUMMON YOUR PET!

JAWOHL, HERR DOCTOR.

THE THING PREVIOUSLY KNOWN AS SERGEANT WOLFGANG NEUMANN WORE A RADIO COLLAR THAT DISPENSED PAINFUL ELECTRIC SHOCKS WHEN HE DISOBEYED.

SAG HALLO ZU DEM PROFESSOR, WOLFGANG!

BUT WAITING FOR THEM INSIDE...

AROOO!

DAMN! FIGURES THEY'D USE ONE AS A GUARD DOG! BRACE YOURSELF, LADS.

AIM FOR THE HEAD!

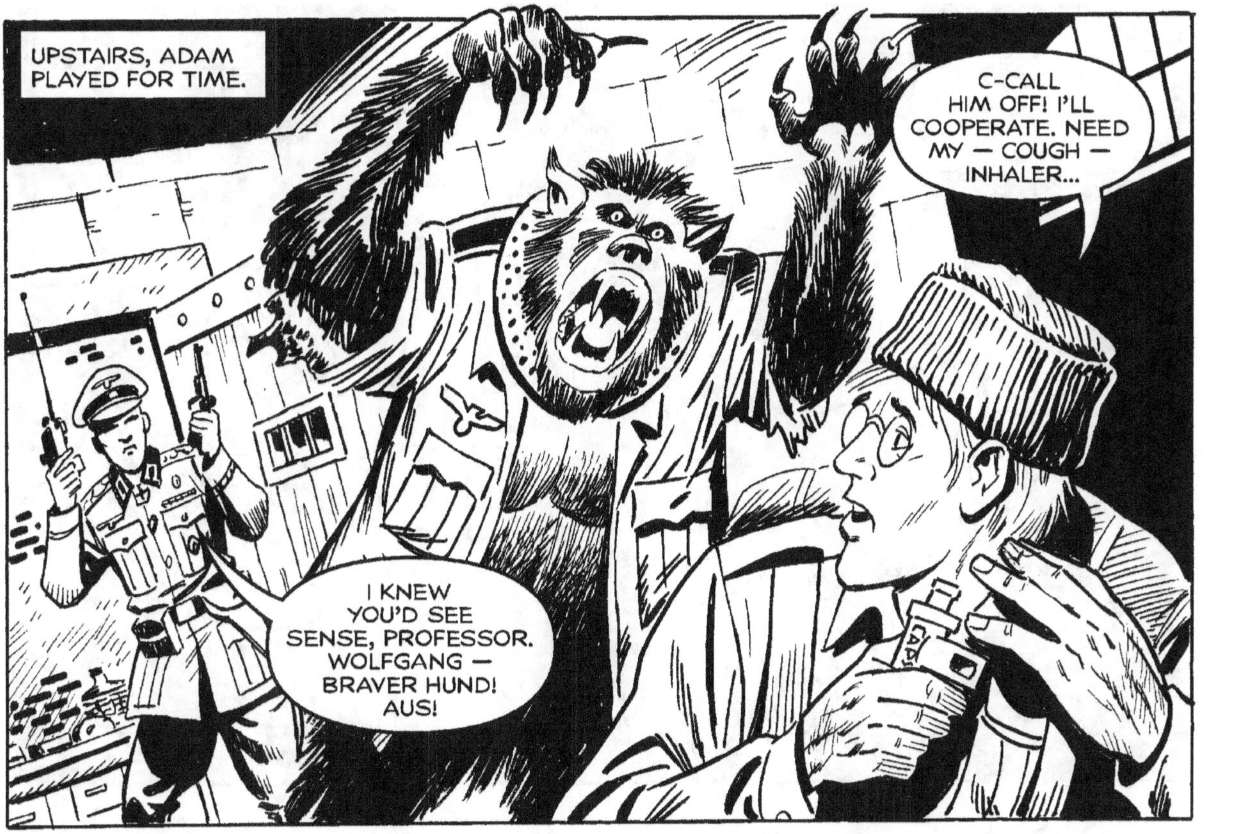

UPSTAIRS, ADAM PLAYED FOR TIME.

C-CALL HIM OFF! I'LL COOPERATE. NEED MY — COUGH — INHALER...

I KNEW YOU'D SEE SENSE, PROFESSOR. WOLFGANG — BRAVER HUND! AUS!

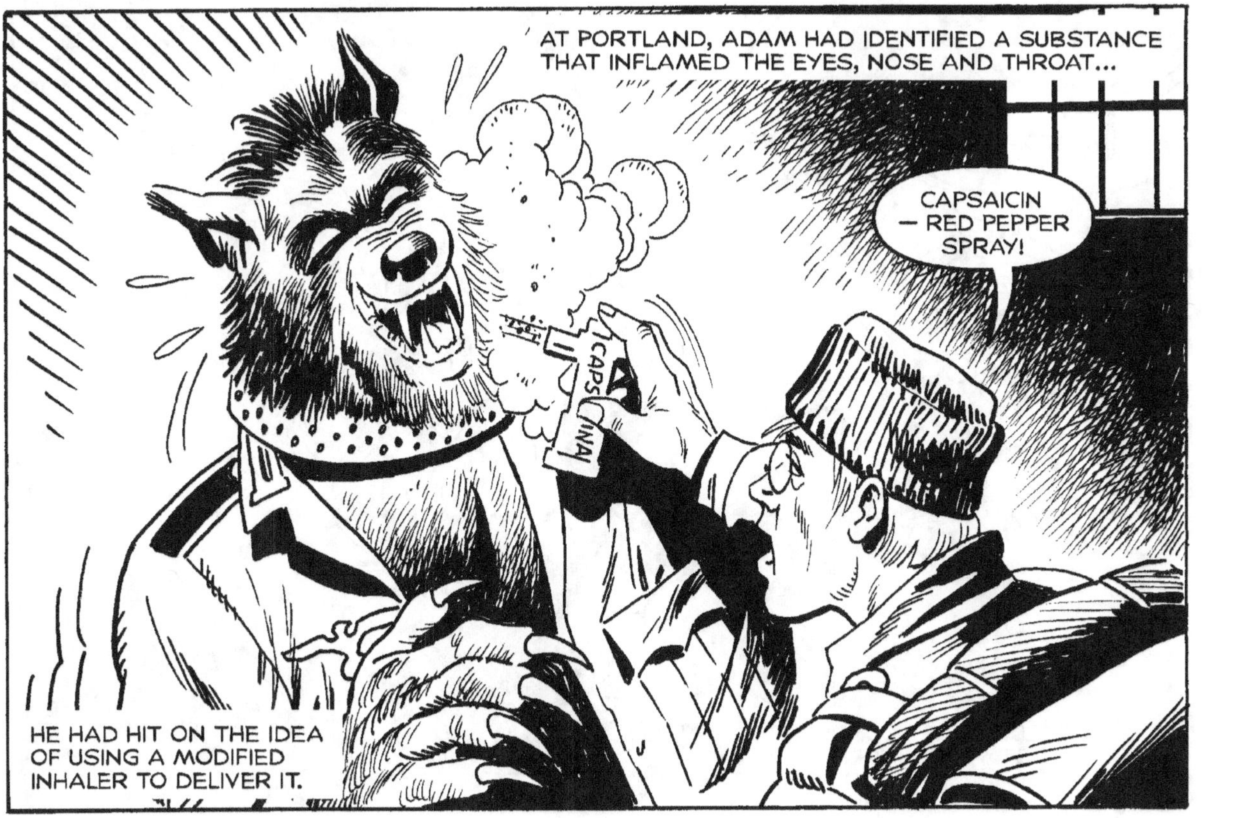

AT PORTLAND, ADAM HAD IDENTIFIED A SUBSTANCE THAT INFLAMED THE EYES, NOSE AND THROAT...

CAPSAICIN — RED PEPPER SPRAY!

HE HAD HIT ON THE IDEA OF USING A MODIFIED INHALER TO DELIVER IT.

CAUSES TEMPORARY BLINDNESS AND SHORTNESS OF BREATH —
ACHTUNG
ACH, USELESS SWINE!

WELCOME TO MY WORLD!
NGH!
ALARM BELLS WERE SOUNDING. SHOUTS, DISTANT GUNFIRE. FOR A MOMENT, ADAM DARED TO HOPE.

HE TRIED TO FOLLOW THE ADVICE HE HAD GIVEN THE OTHERS: STAY CALM AND IN CONTROL, USE YOUR BRAIN.

VERY CLEVER OF BROOKS. GALTON'S WHISTLE — INVENTED IN EIGHTEEN-SEVENTY-SIX AND BETTER KNOWN AS A SILENT DOG WHISTLE.

I SEE THAT GOT YOUR ATTENTION.

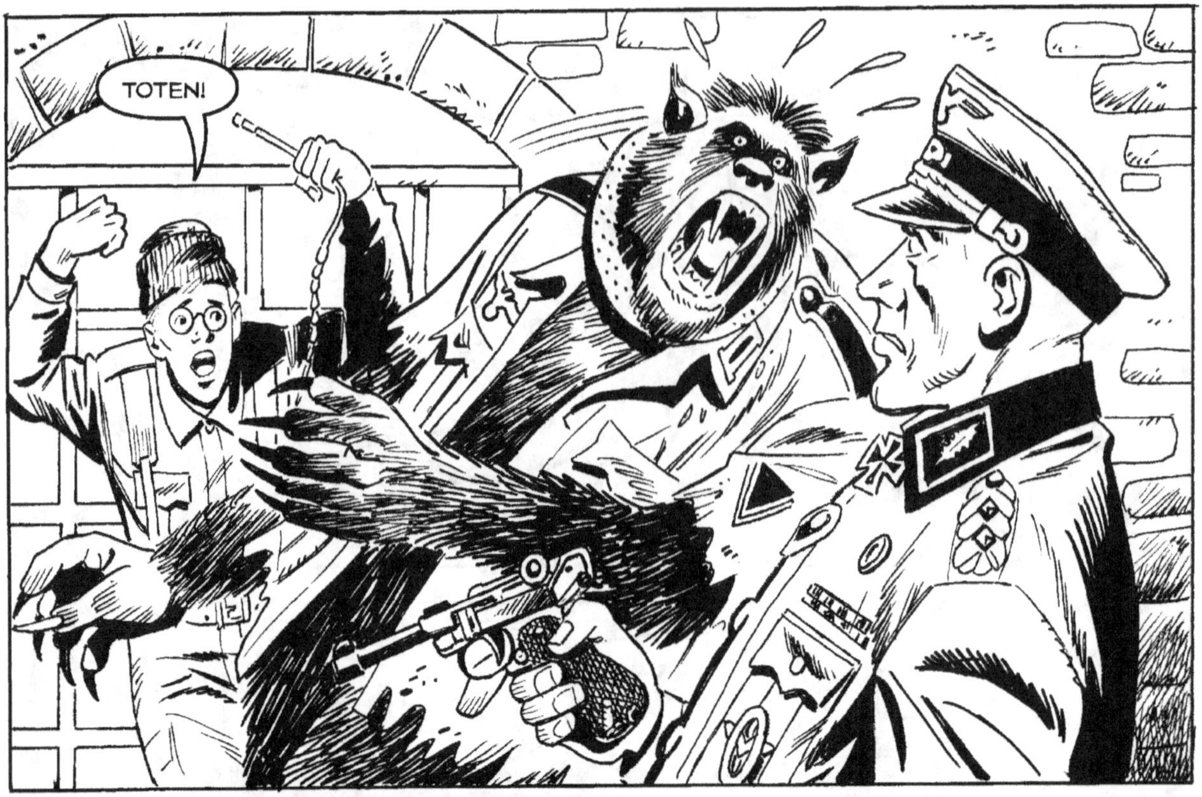
TOTEN!

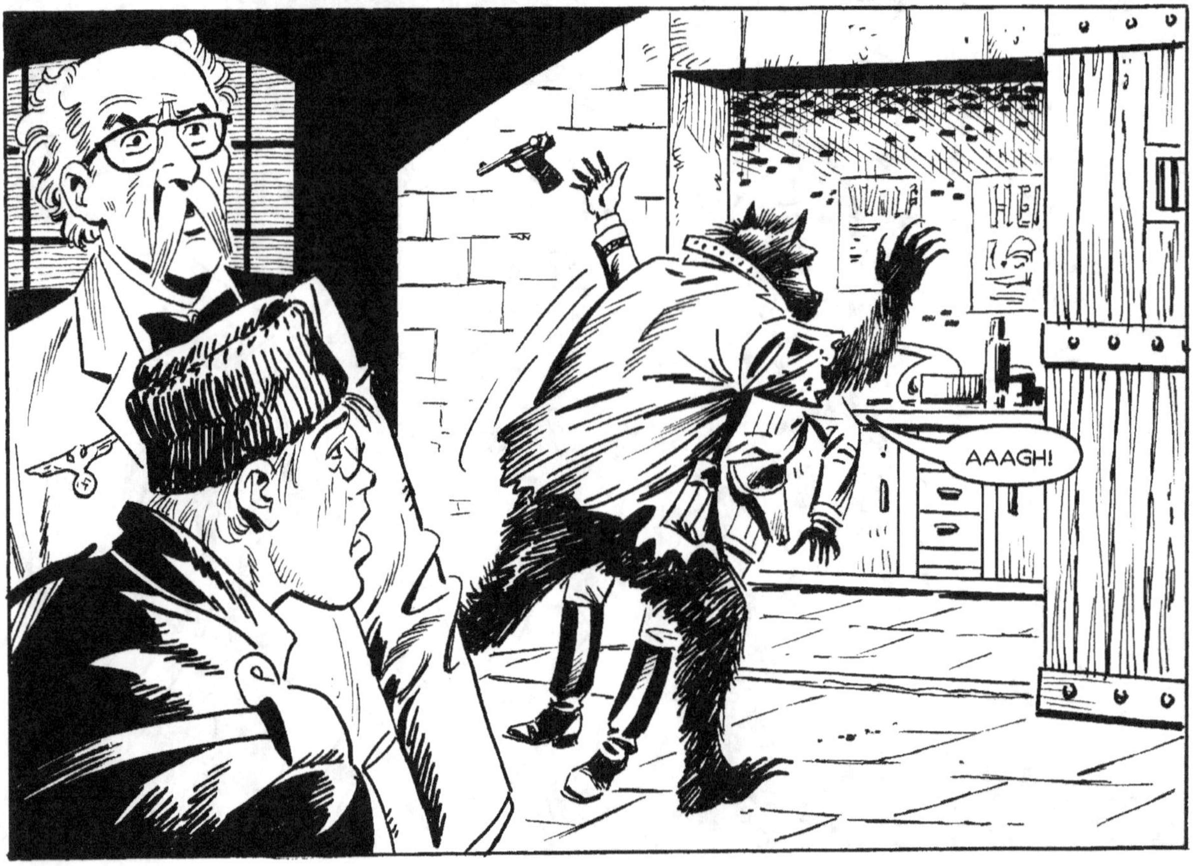
AAAGH!

YOU FOOL! WHAT HAVE YOU DONE?!

NO, WHAT HAVE YOU DONE? YOU'RE A DOCTOR — YOU SHOULD BE CURING DISEASES — NOT CREATING MONSTERS!

WEISE WAS UNSTABLE — A FANATIC — THERE WAS NO REASONING WITH HIM.

YOU THINK YOU'RE BETTER THAN ME — MORE INTELLIGENT! YOU'RE NOT!

AAGH!

I'LL TURN YOU INTO ONE OF THEM — A WOLF!

179

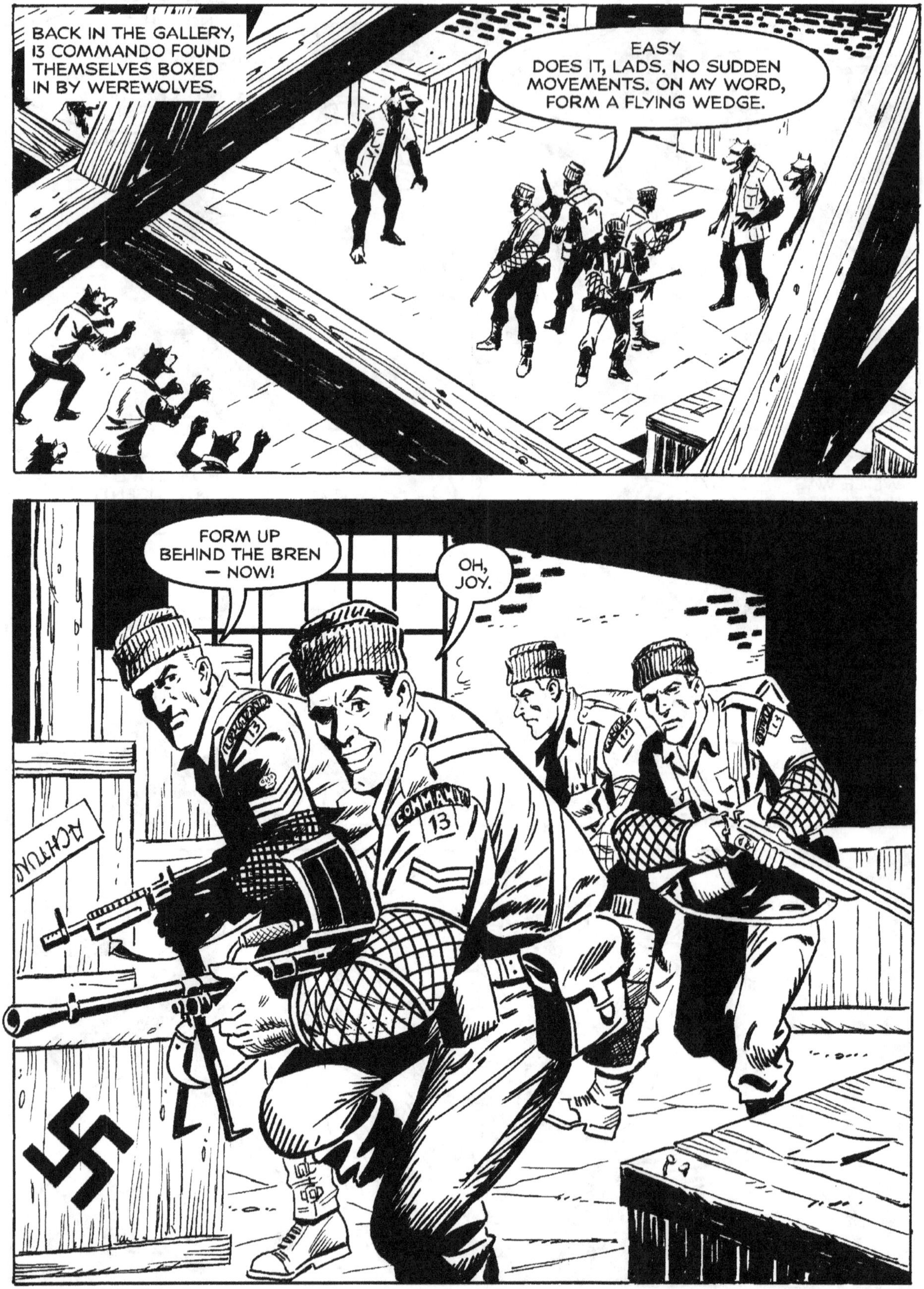

BACK IN THE GALLERY, 13 COMMANDO FOUND THEMSELVES BOXED IN BY WEREWOLVES.

EASY DOES IT, LADS. NO SUDDEN MOVEMENTS. ON MY WORD, FORM A FLYING WEDGE.

FORM UP BEHIND THE BREN — NOW!

OH, JOY.

DON'T LET 'EM GET BEHIND US!

STAFFIE HELD THE OTHER SIDE, COVERING TOTO WHILE THEY RELOADED THE BREN.

STAY IN FORMATION! KEEP IN STEP, LADS — SLOWLY MOVE TOWARDS THE DOOR!

A WOLF'S SENSES ARE FAR KEENER THAN A HUMAN'S. THE LIGHT AND NOISE DISORIENTATED THEM, AS ADAM HAD INTENDED.

WHILE THEY'RE STUNNED — GO!

DOWN, POOCH!

DOOR'S LOCKED!

NOT ANY MORE, IT AIN'T!
COMMANDO
13

ENGLANDERS — UURGH!
OH, FOR CRYING OUT LOUD! NOW WHAT?

THROUGH THERE! HURRY!
WE'LL LET THE WOLVES TAKE CARE OF 'EM!

RARRGH!
N-NEIN!

EVERYONE OKAY? SECURE THE DOOR AND RELOAD!
I'M SWEATING IN PLACES I DIDN'T THINK I COULD SWEAT!

SO THIS IS WHERE THEY MAKE THOSE THINGS. A RUDDY WOLF FACTORY!
COMMANDO
13

MEANWHILE, ADAM WAS PINNED DOWN, UNABLE TO REACH ANY OF HIS GADGETS.

A WOLF! I'LL TURN YOU INTO A WOLF!

G-GET OFF ME, YOU MANIAC!

THE WOLFMAN, HALF-BLINDED AND CONFUSED, COULD SMELL ADAM'S BLOOD ON THE SCALPEL.

NEIN! WHAT ARE YOU —

THWEET!

...WHISTLE?

RRRGH?

STAFFIE WAS OUT OF AMMO, BUT HE RAN AT THE WOLFMAN WITH NO REGARD FOR HIS OWN SAFETY.

OI, RIN-TIN-TIN! PICK ON SOMEONE YOUR OWN SIZE!

CAREFUL, SERGEANT! EVERY PACK HAS ITS ALPHA MALE!

THE TWO SERGEANTS BATTLED IT OUT.

ONLY ROOM FOR ONE TOP DOG HERE, PAL!

DAMMIT, STAFFIE! I CAN'T GET A CLEAR SHOT!

THE WOLFMAN'S TEETH SANK INTO HIS ARM-GUARD, BUT IT HELD.

DESPITE HIS BRAVADO, IT TOOK ALL STAFFIE'S STRENGTH TO HOLD IT AT BAY.

ITS SNOUT IS SENSITIVE! HIT ITS SNOUT!

GERROFF!

THE CREATURE WAS TOO BIG — TOO STRONG — FOR ADAM TO TAKE ON, BUT ITS COLLAR CONTAINED ELECTRICAL EQUIPMENT.

THE TOOLS THAT HAD WEIGHED HIM DOWN EARLIER NOW HAD A PURPOSE AS HE JAMMED THE SCREWDRIVER INTO WOLFGANG'S COLLAR, SHORTING IT OUT.

GRRRGH!

AM I — COUGH — GLAD TO SEE YOU, STAFF SERGEANT!
CALL ME "STAFFIE"... PROF.

WHAT HAPPENED TO BROOKS?
HE WAS WORKING FOR THE GERMANS, BUT THEY DOUBLE-CROSSED HIM. HE WAS THE ONE WHO SET THE WOLVES ON YOU.
ER, LADS. ABOUT THOSE CHARGES I SET...
TIME WE SCARPERED!

GET SHOT, GET EXPLODED OR GET RUNNING, NAZIS!
GOTT IN HIMMEL!

AAIIEE!

WHEN THE CHIPS WERE DOWN, THE ENEMY HAD TURNED ON ONE ANOTHER. ADAM KNEW THEY COULD BEAT THEM IF THEY STUCK TOGETHER.

THEIR SECRET WEAPON WAS THEIR DETERMINATION AND UNITY.

AS THEY TREKKED BACK DOWN THROUGH THE WOODS, THE FOG LIFTED AND THE MOON NO LONGER SEEMED QUITE SO MENACING.

YOU KNOW, GADGETS AND INVENTIONS ARE UNIMPORTANT — IT'S THE MEN WHO WEAR THEM THAT COUNT.

OH YEAH? WELL, I'VE GOT SOME IDEAS HOW WE MIGHT MAKE THESE A BIT MORE PRACTICAL...

NIGHT WITCH

German soldiers feared the night. Their restless sleep was interrupted by a sound caught on the wind — like the flapping of wings or the knocking of flying broomsticks. Like ghosts, the Polikarpov Po-2 fighters of 588th Night Bomber Regiment swooped in to attack, destroying all that dared to be in their path. The Germans soon began to call these fearsome female pilots 'The Nachthexen' — The Night Witches...

However, there was more to one of these women than there seemed.

Commando
THE HOME OF HEROES
www.commandocomics.com

COMPLETE 63-PAGE ACTION STORY

Commando

60 YEARS

EST. 1961

THE HOME OF HEROES

NIGHT WITCH

HARRIS

Story: Georgia Standen Battle

Originally from London, Georgia Standen Battle is a DC Thomson comics staffer, working on titles such as *Commando, Beano, The Dandy, The Broons* and *Oor Wullie*. Battle started her career at Titan Comics but, once established at DC Thomson, wrote her first issue #5229 'The Shadow in the Sky' making her the first woman to have written for *Commando* since the 1980s. Since then Battle has written over 10 *Commandos* including the 'Commandos vs Zombies' series, the third of which came out for Halloween 2022.

Art: Vicente Alcazar

Born in Madrid in 1944, Vicente Alcazar is a Spanish artist who started his career in the 1960s. Alcazar has worked on Archie Comics, Red Circle Comics, DC Comics and Marvel Comics. He is well-known for horror comics and his run on *Jonah Hex*. Alcazar collaborated with fellow *Commando* artist Carlos Pino under the portmanteau pseudonym CARVIC, working on war comics for *Chico* and *War Picture Library*. Despite this, his first *Commando* wasn't until 2015. Since then Alcazar has become a regular contributor to *Commando* with many issues taking advantage of his background in horror artwork.

Cover: Mark Harris

Canadian Mark Harris is a new addition to the *Commando* roster. Harris' first ever *Commando* cover was for the 60th Anniversary of the title on #5454 'The Avengers' in 2021. Since then, Harris has lent his skill to 14 *Commandos* during 2021 to 2022 and has cemented himself as one of the leading cover artists of the modern *Commando* era.

NIGHT WITCH

THE WOMEN FLYERS AND NAVIGATORS OF THE 588TH NIGHT BOMBER REGIMENT WERE FIERCE FIGHTERS, THEIR SILENT NIGHT BOMBING TACTICS WREAKING HAVOC AMONG THE GERMAN LINES.

STORY
GEORGIA STANDEN BATTLE

ART
VICENTE ALCAZAR

COVER
MARK HARRIS

THEIR METHODS EARNED THEM A NICKNAME AMONGST THE ENEMY TROOPS, THE 'NACHTHEXEN' OR NIGHT WITCHES.

WHEN HITLER BETRAYED HIS ALLIES AND INVADED THE USSR, THE RED ARMY WAS CAUGHT BY SURPRISE.

BUT THE WHOLE OF THE SOVIET UNION WAS READY TO STAND AGAINST THE NAZI INVADERS, AND WOMEN, AS WELL AS MEN, ENLISTED TO FIGHT.

ALTHOUGH WOMEN HAD INITIALLY BEEN REFUSED ENTRY INTO THE AIR FORCE, THE SOVIET UNION'S OWN 'AMELIA EARHART', MARINA RASKOVA, USED HER FAME AND PERSONAL CONTACTS WITH JOSEPH STALIN TO PETITION THE CREATION OF AN ALL-FEMALE UNIT.

HOWEVER, NOT EVERYONE WAS RESPECTFUL OF THE FEMALE PILOTS AND NAVIGATORS. POSTED TO AN AIRFIELD ALONGSIDE ALL-MALE UNITS, THE MEN VIEWED THEM AS INFERIOR FLYERS AND AS PROPAGANDA.

THE WOMEN WERE GIVEN RUDIMENTARY TOOLS AND EQUIPMENT AS WELL AS HAND-ME-DOWN UNIFORMS, WHICH WERE TOO BIG AND DESIGNED FOR MEN — EVEN DOWN TO THE UNDERGARMENTS.

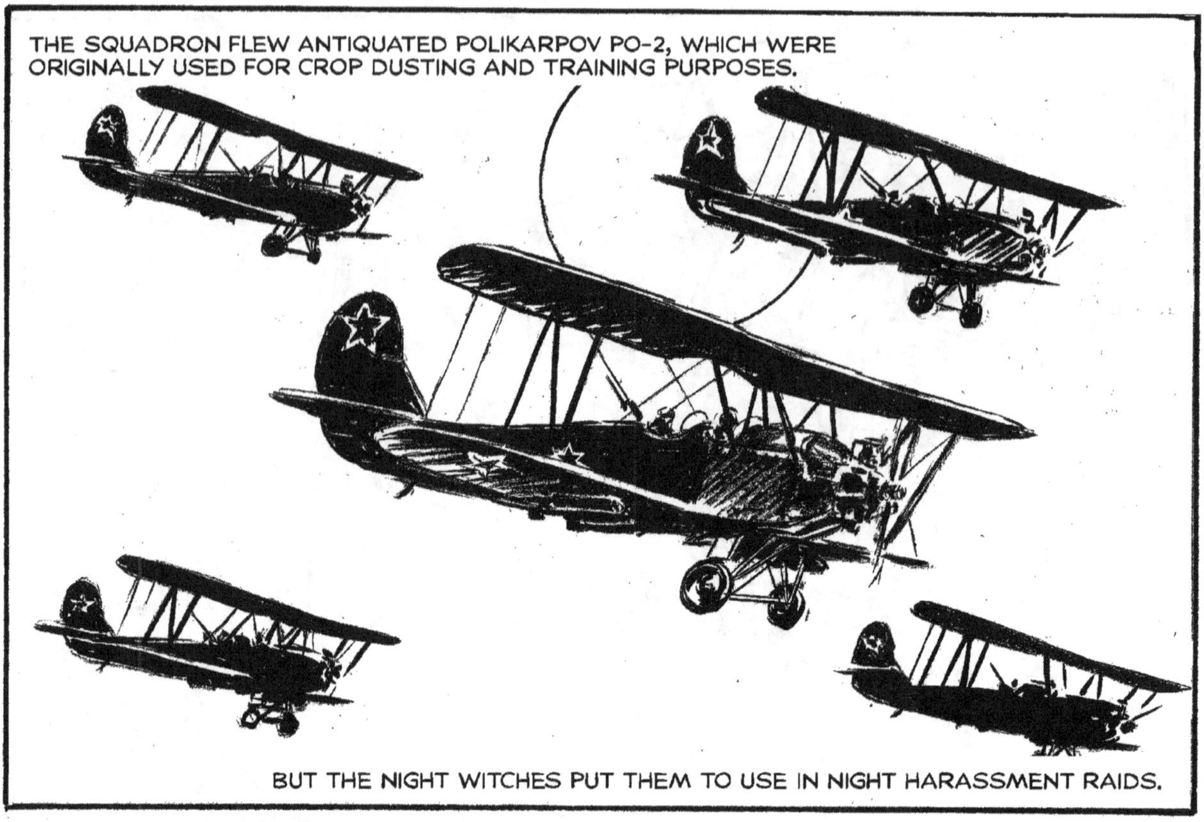

THE SQUADRON FLEW ANTIQUATED POLIKARPOV PO-2, WHICH WERE ORIGINALLY USED FOR CROP DUSTING AND TRAINING PURPOSES.

BUT THE NIGHT WITCHES PUT THEM TO USE IN NIGHT HARASSMENT RAIDS.

THEY SOON EARNED A DREADED REPUTATION.

WITH THEM AROUND, THE GERMANS HAD MANY SLEEPLESS NIGHTS, FEARING THE WITCHES WOULD ATTACK.

INSIDE ONE PO-2, WAS IRINA POPOVA. BEFORE THE WAR SHE HAD BEEN A TEACHER AT AN AVIATION SCHOOL AND WAS WELL USED TO FLYING.

HOW LONG LEFT, VERA?

NOT LONG. WE ARE NEARLY TO THE TARGET. ANOTHER COLD NIGHT IN A SEWING MACHINE, HUH?

SEWING MACHINE WAS THE AFFECTIONATE NICKNAME THE WOMEN OF THE 588TH HAD GIVEN TO THE PO-2.

IRINA'S NAVIGATOR AND BOMBARDIER WAS VERA SMIRNOVA, A WHIP-SMART, WITTY YOUNG WOMAN WHO HAD GRADUATED FROM THE UNIVERSITY OF MOSCOW WITH A DEGREE IN MECHANICS AND MATHEMATICS.

HOW MANY SORTIES HAVE YOU FLOWN NOW, IRINA? YOU MUST BE OVER THREE-HUNDRED BY NOW?

TOO MANY TO COUNT.

IRINA COULD BE A WOMAN OF FEW WORDS BUT THE PAIR WERE GOOD FRIENDS AND A BALANCED TEAM.

DESPITE HAVING ONLY BEEN ON THE FRONT LINES FOR ABOUT A YEAR, IRINA HAD ACCUMULATED OVER 350 MISSIONS. ALTHOUGH SHE WOULD NOT TELL ANYONE, IRINA FELT THE STRAIN ON HER NERVES GROW EVERY FLIGHT.

YOU HONESTLY DON'T KNOW HOW MANY YOU'VE FLOWN? NINA RYABOVA HAS A CHART...

I DON'T CARE ABOUT WHAT NINA DOES. SHE HAS COTTON FLUFF IN HER SKULL.

BIT HARSH!

ENOUGH TALKING. WE MUST BE SILENT OR THE ENEMY WILL HEAR US. YOU KNOW THAT.

SHE IS TOUCHY TONIGHT AGAIN. SHE COULD DO WITH SOME REST FOR ONCE.

THE SQUADRON FLEW SEVERAL SORTIES A NIGHT TO DISRUPT THE GERMANS AS MUCH AS POSSIBLE.

THE WEIGHT OF THEIR BOMBS FORCED THEM TO FLY AT LOW ALTITUDES WHICH MADE THEIR RAIDS DANGEROUS AND THE WOMEN EASY TARGETS.

ONCE THEY WERE APPROACHING THE TARGET, VERA TAPPED IRINA ON THE SHOULDER. THIS WAS THE SIGNAL TO CUT THE ENGINE.

THE NACHTHEXEN HAD DEVELOPED A VERY PARTICULAR TACTIC FOR THEIR BOMBING RAIDS.

WITH THE ENGINE OFF OR IDLING, THE PO-2 WOULD GLIDE IN TO MAKE THE ATTACK RUN.

IT WAS A RISKY MOVE, AS THEY WOULD HAVE TO HOPE THEIR AIRCRAFT'S ENGINE WOULD TURN BACK ON AGAIN ONCE THEIR BOMBING WAS OVER.

ON THE GROUND, THE SLEEPY GERMAN SOLDIERS HAD NO IDEA WHAT WAS COMING.

PASS ME THE COFFEE, KAMERAD.

NEIN, THERE IS NONE LEFT. YOU MUST MAKE MORE IF YOU WANT IT.

I'M NOT MAKING IT. YOU MAKE —

SHUT UP! DON'T YOU HEAR THAT?

WHAT THE GERMAN COULD HEAR WAS THE WIND WHISTLING THROUGH THE WOODEN FRAME OF THE PO-2. THE ONLY INDICATION THAT SOMETHING WICKED WAS COMING THEIR WAY.

BECAUSE THE PO-2 WERE SMALL AND FLYING AT LOW ALTITUDE, THEY DID NOT SHOW UP ON RADAR, AND THEY DID NOT HAVE OR USE RADIO SO THEY COULDN'T BE TRACKED BY THAT EITHER. THE WOMEN WERE LIKE GHOSTS.

THE WITCHES TRAVELLED IN GROUPS — OR COVENS, WITH THE FIRST PO-2 ACTING AS BAIT. THEY WOULD DROP A FLARE ON THE INTENDED TARGET AND DRAW THE ATTENTION OF THE GERMAN SPOTLIGHTS TO ILLUMINATE THE BASE SO IT COULD BE ATTACKED.

AFTER GLIDING IN THE DARK, VERA DROPPED THEIR DEADLY PAYLOAD.

THE NACHTHEXEN!

THE CARNAGE BEGAN. THE GERMAN SOLDIERS SCATTERED AS BOMBS EXPLODED.

THE WITCHES LAID DEVASTATION IN THEIR WAKE, THEIR PAYLOADS DESTROYING EQUIPMENT AND TROOPS.

THE PO-2 FLEW AWAY FROM THE CHAOS IT HAD WROUGHT ON THE GERMANS. VERA WAS JUBILANT AT ANOTHER JOB WELL DONE.

BOZHE MOI, THAT ONE WENT UP LIKE A CATHERINE WHEEL. WELL DONE, COMRADE.

CONGRATULATE ME WHEN WE ARE IN OUR BEDS SAFE, VERA. FOR NOW, WE RETURN TO BASE. WE'VE GOT ANOTHER RUN BEFORE THE NIGHT IS OUT.

THE 588TH OFTEN FLEW SEVERAL SORTIES A NIGHT TO KEEP THE GERMANS HARRIED. WORKING AS THEIR OWN GROUND CREW AND MECHANICS, THEY WOULD REFUEL, HANG NEW BOMBS AND FLY OFF AGAIN.

IRINA! OVER HERE!

IRINA AND VERA LANDED AFTER THEIR LAST SORTIE OF THE NIGHT WHEN KATYA IVANOV CAME TO GREET THEM.

BACK FROM ANOTHER NIGHT OF CASTING SPELLS ON THE NAZIS?

DROPPING OUR CAULDRONS ON SOME HITLERITE HEADS, YOU MEAN?

HA! IF I EVER MET HITLER, I'D STICK MY BROOMSTICK WHERE —
KATYA!
IRINA AND KATYA WERE GOOD FRIENDS, HAVING GONE THROUGH TRAINING AT ENGELS MILITARY SCHOOL OF AVIATION TOGETHER.

I'M GLAD YOU MADE IT BACK SAFE.
YOU TOO, KATYA.
YOU LOOK TERRIBLE, THOUGH. GET SOME REST.
THAT'S WHAT I KEEP TELLING HER.

THE WOMEN SLEPT DURING THE DAY, WAITING UNTIL PITCH-BLACK NIGHT BEFORE BEGINNING THEIR MISSIONS AGAIN.

IRINA WAS EXHAUSTED, HER NERVES WERE PULLED TIGHT LIKE ELASTIC SHE WORRIED WOULD SNAP. SHE TRIED HARD TO GET TO SLEEP.

WHEN IT FINALLY CAME, THE REST WAS FITFUL AND HER DREAMS HARROWING.

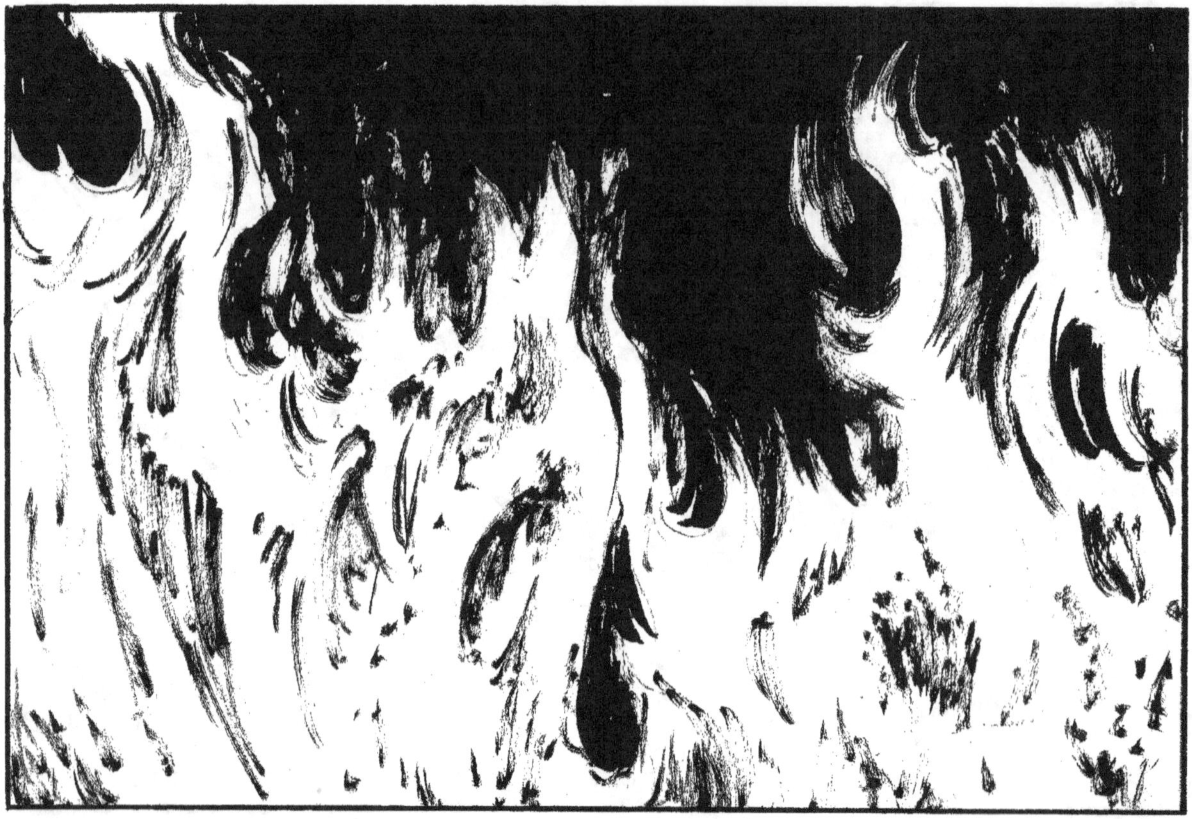

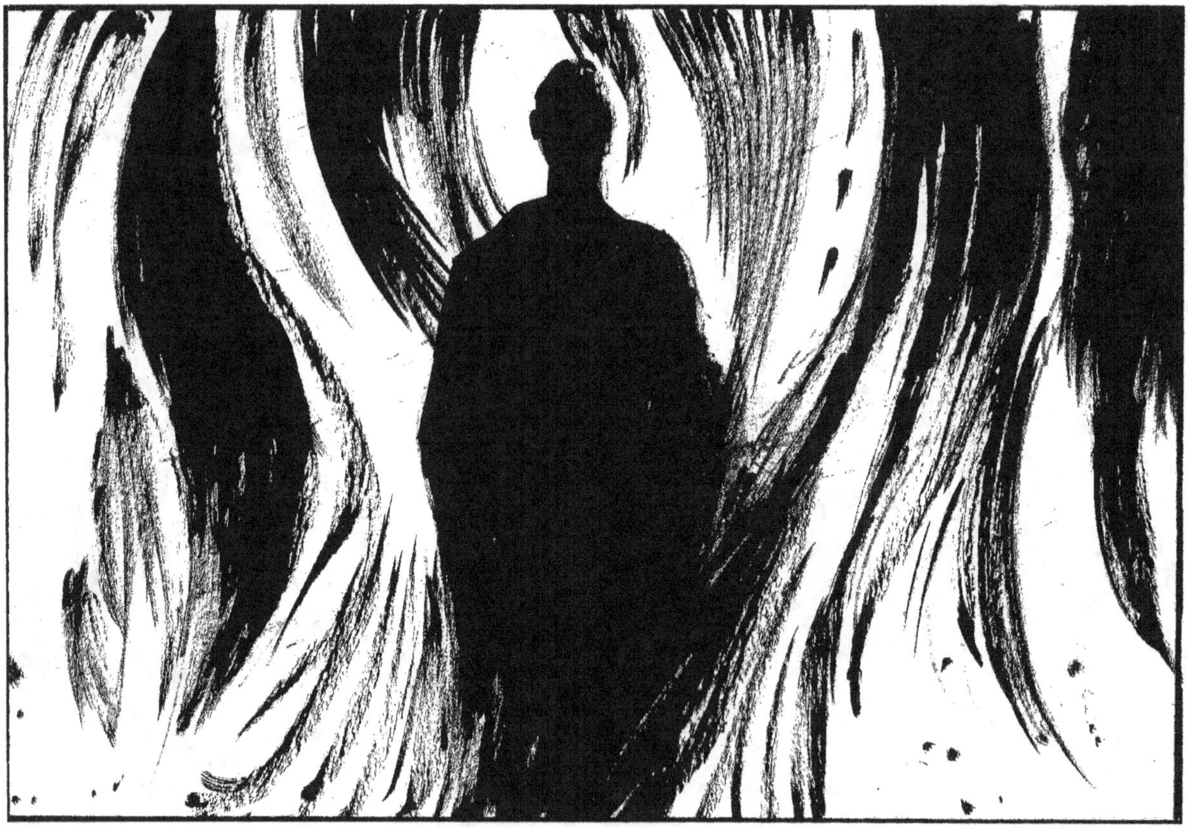

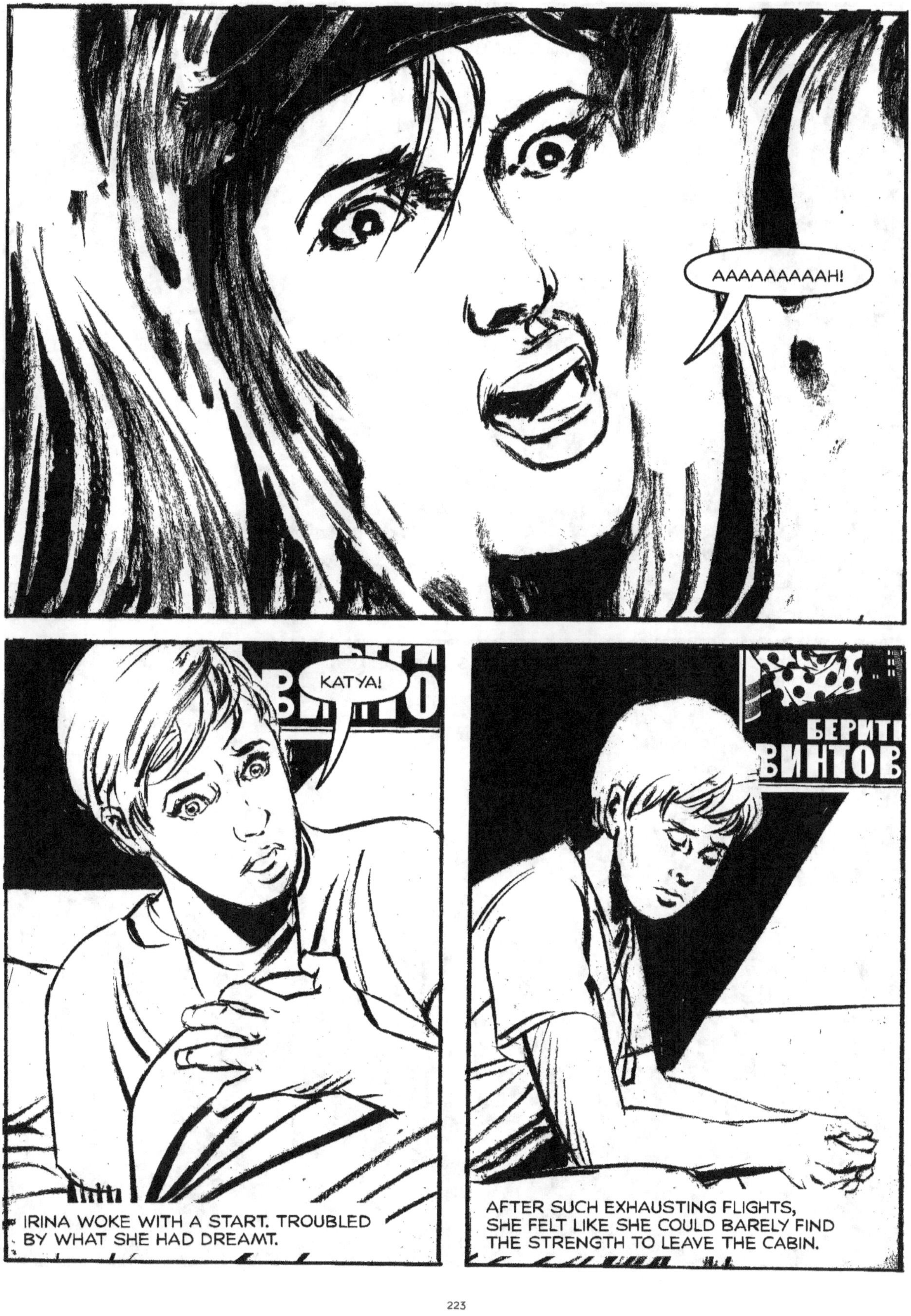

IRINA WOKE WITH A START. TROUBLED BY WHAT SHE HAD DREAMT.

AFTER SUCH EXHAUSTING FLIGHTS, SHE FELT LIKE SHE COULD BARELY FIND THE STRENGTH TO LEAVE THE CABIN.

SOON THEY WERE UP AND ABOUT AGAIN. THIS TIME THEIR OBJECTIVE WAS TO DESTROY A RIVER CROSSING BUILT BY THE GERMANS.

LITTLE DID THE WITCHES KNOW, THE AREA WAS DEFENDED BY GERMAN ANTI-AIRCRAFT GUNS.

ENEMY AIRCRAFT SIGHTED.

KATYA'S PO-2 WAS THE FIRST TO MAKE THE BOMBING RUN.

BABA YAGA IS COMING FOR YOU, NAZIS.

THE CREWS OF THE AA GUNS WORKED FURIOUSLY, AND SOON THEY BEGAN BOOMING.

FEUER!

KATYA BEGAN HER RUN, IGNORING THE BLACK PUFFS OF COTTON EXPLODING AROUND HER.

THE FLAK WAS TOO THICK, AND SOON IT BEGAN EXPLODING CLOSER AND CLOSER TOWARDS THE FRAGILE WOODEN AIRCRAFT.

KATYA? KATYA?!

KATYA'S NAVIGATOR, POLINA MAKAROVA'S CALLS WENT UNHEARD, KATYA HAD BEEN KILLED.

WITH EYES BLINDED BY TEARS, POLINA TOOK CONTROL OF THE PO-2 AND ATTEMPTED TO FLY IT HOME.

MEANWHILE, THE RAID CONTINUED, WITH ANOTHER WITCH TAKING AIM AT THE RIVER CROSSING.

THE BOMB HIT ITS MARK, SPLINTERING THE BRIDGE WITH LETHAL FORCE.

IRINA AND VERA CAME IN TO LAND BUT WERE SHOCKED WHEN THEY WERE NOT GREETED BY THEIR FRIEND.
WHERE'S KATYA?
INSTINCTIVELY, IRINA KNEW SOMETHING WAS WRONG, DEATHLY WRONG.

KATYA?
IRINA! WHERE ARE YOU GOING? WE HAVE ANOTHER RUN TO MAKE!

IRINA RUSHED OVER TO ANOTHER PO-2. THE TWO WOMEN IN THE AIRCRAFT LOOKED AT HER, CONFUSED.

KATYA?

QUICKLY, SHE RAN TO ANOTHER AIRCRAFT.

KATYA?

SORRY. HAVEN'T SEEN HER.

FINALLY, IRINA FOUND KATYA'S PO-2.
POLINA! WHAT'S GOING ON? WHERE IS KATYA?
OH, IRINA...

KATYA...

IRINA LET THE TEARS RUN FROM HER EYES, TRYING TO DISPEL THE EMOTIONS THAT HAD BEEN CONJURED UP INSIDE HER. BUT TRY AS SHE MIGHT, SHE FELT THE BURNING HATRED IGNITE INSIDE HER SOUL.

I'LL MAKE THEM PAY. EVERY NAZI IN THE SOVIET UNION WILL PAY FOR THIS.

SHE HAD A JOB TO DO, ANOTHER SORTIE TO FLY. VERA SAW THE EXPRESSION ON HER FACE AND TRIED TO COMFORT HER.

KATYA? IS SHE?

SHE IS — SHE IS DEAD.

POOR THING. I'M SO SORRY.

WE'LL AVENGE HER. I PROMISE.

IRINA REMEMBERED HER DREAM, KATYA CALLING OUT IN PAIN. SUDDENLY, SHE COULD NOT SHAKE THE FEELING SHE HAD SEEN THE FUTURE.

ALTHOUGH THEY GRIEVED FOR THEIR FRIEND, THE PAIR WERE BACK ON MISSIONS. ONE NIGHT, THEY WERE TO DROP MUCH NEEDED SUPPLIES TO RED ARMY TROOPS.

IT WAS A QUIET NIGHT COMPARED TO SOME OF THEIR OTHER SORTIES.

THE PAIR FELT GOOD, KNOWING THEY WERE HELPING PEOPLE TO SURVIVE.

BUT THERE WAS SOMETHING BREWING IN THE NIGHT, AND THINGS WERE ABOUT TO HEAT UP FOR THEM.

THEY HAD BEEN SPOTTED BY AN ENEMY NIGHT FIGHTER.

A BIPLANE? MAYBE IT IS ONE OF THE DREADED NACHTHEXEN. I COULD EARN MYSELF A MEDAL.

ACCORDING TO SOME, DOWNING A NIGHT WITCH AWARDED AN AUTOMATIC IRON CROSS FOR A LUFTWAFFE AIRMAN.

IRINA! WE'VE GOT COMPANY! NIGHT FIGHTER COMING THIS WAY.

HELLFIRE! THAT'S JUST WHAT WE NEED!

THE GERMAN BEGAN HIS ATTACK BUT WAS ANNOYED TO SEE HIS BULLET BUZZ HARMLESSLY PAST THE RUSSIAN AIRCRAFT.

TEUFEL!

IRINA HAD CLEVERLY SLOWED DOWN HER PLANE, KNOWING THAT THE PO-2 COULD FLY SLOWER THAN THE STALLING SPEED OF THE ENEMY NIGHT FIGHTER.

VERA TOOK ADVANTAGE, PEPPERING THE ENEMY'S BELLY WITH BULLETS.

HOW DO YOU LIKE THIS WICKED WITCH, NAZI?!

VERDAMMT, WITCHES!

I HAVE YOU NOW!

IRINA TURNED THE PO-2 — USING ITS EXCEPTIONAL MANOEUVRABILITY TO DODGE THE NIGHT FIGHTER'S BULLETS ONCE AGAIN.
NEIN!
NOT TODAY, SATAN!

ALTHOUGH THE RUSSIAN BIPLANE WAS OLD, IT WAS NIMBLE. SOON IT WAS ON THE NIGHT FIGHTER'S TAIL.

I'LL MAKE EVERY LAST NAZI PAY FOR WHAT THEY DID TO KATYA.

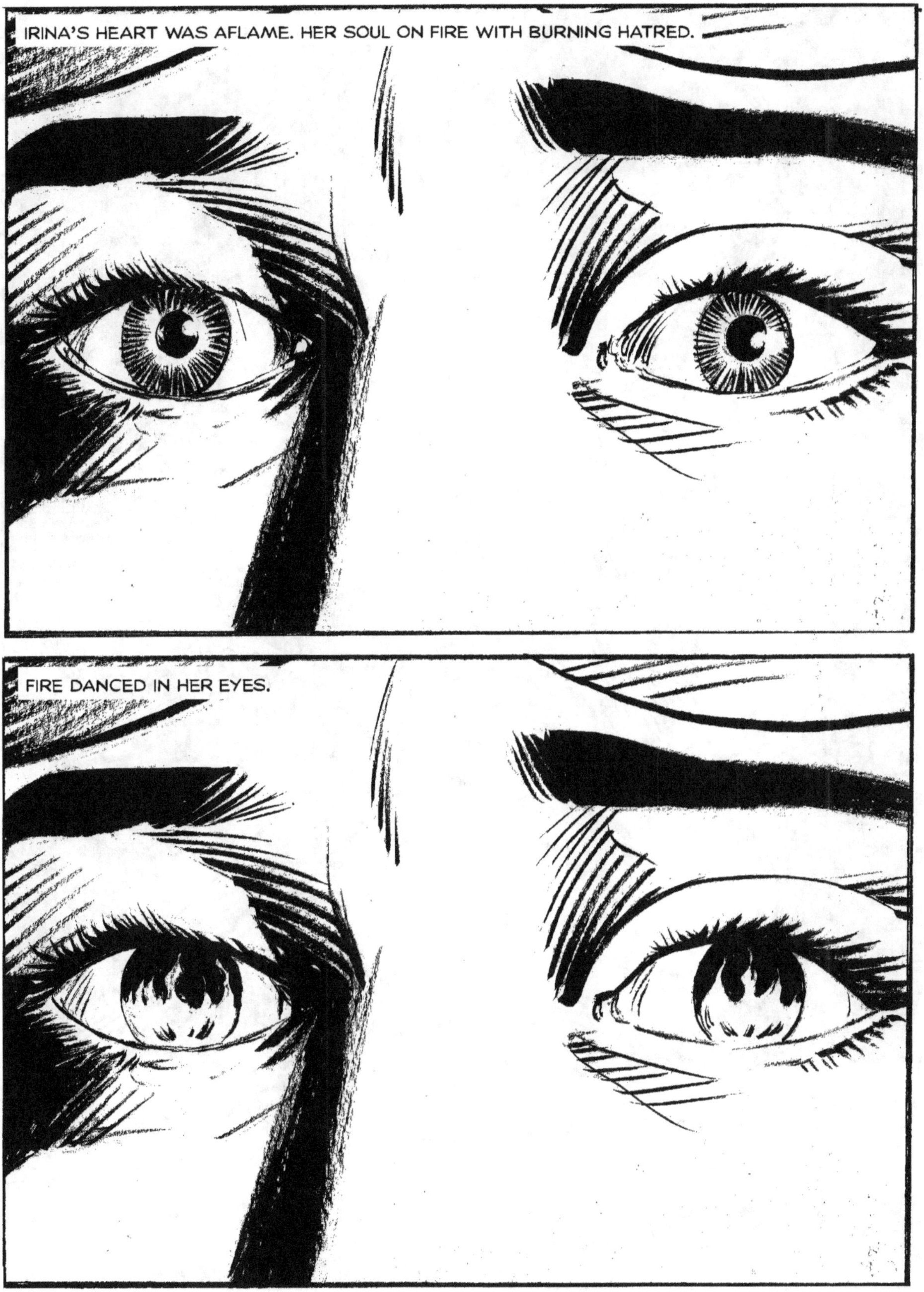

IRINA'S HEART WAS AFLAME. HER SOUL ON FIRE WITH BURNING HATRED.

FIRE DANCED IN HER EYES.

BOZHE MOI!
DID I — DID I DO THAT?

WHAT JUST HAPPENED, VERA? DID YOU SEE WHAT GOT IT?
NYET. MAYBE IT GOT HIT BY ONE OF OUR FLAK GUNS?

I DIDN'T HEAR ANY ANTI-AIRCRAFT FIRE...BUT I FELT SOMETHING. I WANTED IT TO BE ON FIRE, AND THEN IT WAS...

VERA, I HAVE TO TALK TO YOU ABOUT SOMETHING. ABOUT WHAT HAPPENED WITH THAT GERMAN NIGHT FIGHTER.
DA? WHAT ABOUT IT?

I'M SAYING...I THINK I DID IT.

WHAT DO YOU MEAN? HOW COULD YOU HAVE DONE IT?

I WANTED IT TO BE ON FIRE, I WANTED IT TO BURN FOR WHAT THEY DID TO KATYA. I WANTED THEM TO BE CAUGHT IN AN INFERNO — I WISHED IT, URGED IT IN MY SOUL — AND THEN IT WAS.

ARE YOU SAYING YOU REALLY ARE A WITCH? YOU'VE LOST IT.

LISTEN, I MEAN IT. I FELT A POWER STIRRING INSIDE ME.

246

BUT WHEN SHE WENT TO SLEEP, IRINA COULDN'T JUST FORGET ABOUT IT. IN FACT, SHE REMEMBERED SOMETHING THAT HAD HAPPENED TO HER BEFORE...AND SHE BEGAN TO DREAM OF IT.

BACK WHEN IRINA HAD JUST ENLISTED, AND ON HER LAST NIGHT OF FREEDOM, SHE AND SOME OF HER FRIENDS HAD TAKEN A TRIP INTO THE FOREST TO REVEL.

THEY LIT A BONFIRE TO KEEP THEM WARM WHILE THEY DANCED, DRANK, AND ATE.

IRINA! COME, TAKE YOUR SHOES OFF AND DANCE!

BUT IRINA WAS SCARED. AS SHE STARED INTO THE FIRE, SHE WISHED. SHE WISHED SHE WOULD SURVIVE THE WAR AT ANY COST, WISHED SHE COULD BE GRANTED POWER.

CASTING OFF HER SHOES, SHE LET GO, THROWING HERSELF INTO THE DANCE.

HER EYES SHUT, IRINA DANCED, HOLDING HER FRIENDS' HANDS, HER HEAD TILTED TOWARD THE NIGHT SKY AND THE FIRE.

IN HER HEART SHE KEPT WISHING. WISHING FOR POWER.

AT THE TIME, NO-ONE NOTICED WHAT OR WHO LINGERED IN THE BONFIRE.

IRINA'S EYES SNAPPED OPEN. HER BODY WAS DRENCHED IN SWEAT AND ALTHOUGH SHE HAD BEEN ASLEEP, SHE FELT NO MORE RESTED.

BACK THEN, WAS THERE SOMEONE — SOMETHING IN THE FIRE?

DID I DANCE WITH SOMETHING? WHAT IF I ACCIDENTALLY MADE A DEAL FOR THE POWER TO SURVIVE THE WAR?

IRINA HAD NO TIME TO DWELL AS VERA CAME RUSHING INTO THE CABIN. OUTSIDE WERE THE TELL-TALE SIGNS OF A COMMOTION.

BOZHE MOI, IRINA, YOU LOOK AWFUL. DID YOU NOT GET ANY SLEEP?

NEVER MIND THAT, WHAT'S GOING ON?

WE'RE BEING GROUNDED, COME QUICK.

FOR THE FIRST TIME, THE NIGHT WITCHES WERE REALLY, REALLY NERVOUS. THEY GATHERED ON THE AIRSTRIP TO LISTEN TO THEIR REGIMENT COMMANDER.

FOLLOWING LAST NIGHT'S EVENTS, THE SQUADRON WILL BE GROUNDED FOR ONE WHOLE NIGHT. I SUGGEST YOU TAKE THE TIME TO REGROUP BEFORE SORTIES RESUME TOMORROW.

NYET! WE SHOULD AVENGE NINA, ZOYA AND RAISA!

AND MARIA, ANNA AND ANYA!

SO MANY LOST, VERA? WHAT HAPPENED?

THEY SAID IT WAS A GERMAN PILOT. HE TOOK DOWN THREE OF OUR PLANES IN ONE NIGHT. THEY'RE CALLING HIM THE WITCH HUNTER.

IRINA'S BLOOD WENT COLD. USUALLY, THE NIGHT WITCHES WERE ABLE TO OUTFLY SUCH ATTACKS. NEVER BEFORE HAD SO MANY BEEN LOST ON ONE NIGHT.

WITCH HUNTER? I'M NOT SCARED OF HIM.

THAT MAY BE SO, POPOVA. BUT TAKE THIS TIME TO GET SOME REST. YOU ESPECIALLY LOOK LIKE YOU NEED IT. YOU'RE NO GOOD TIRED — OR DEAD.

THAT NIGHT, IRINA DID GET SOME SLEEP BUT HER DREAMS WERE ONCE AGAIN UNEASY. SHE DREAMT OF FALLING...

...THE GROUND CAME CLOSER AND CLOSER TOWARDS HER.

JUST AS IRINA WAS ABOUT TO HIT THE EARTH, SHE JOLTED AWAKE. SWEAT AND PANIC CLINGING TO HER.

IT WAS A REAL FEAR THE PILOT HELD, FOR THE 588TH RARELY TOOK PARACHUTES WITH THEM BECAUSE OF THE EXTRA WEIGHT.

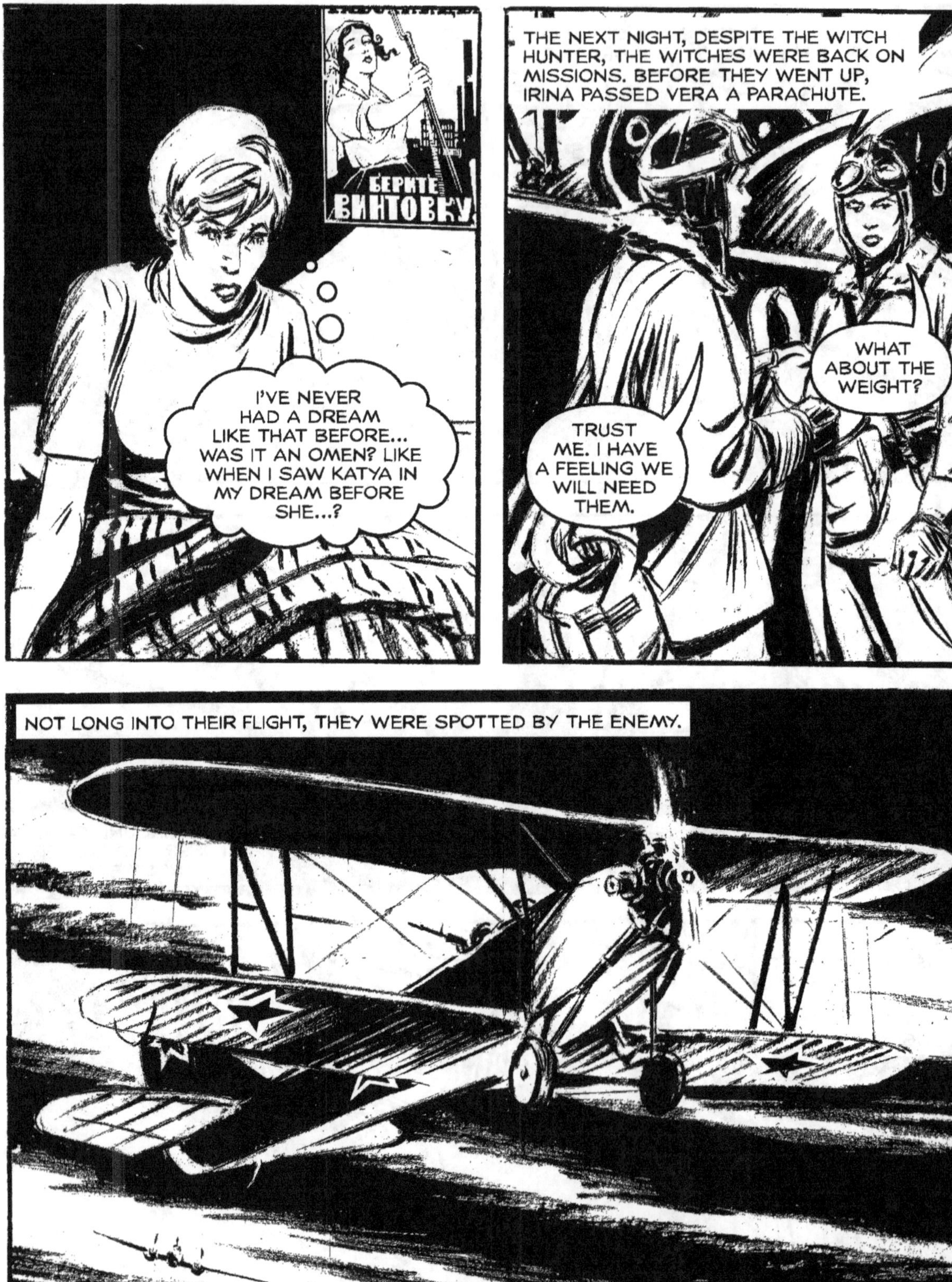

I'VE NEVER HAD A DREAM LIKE THAT BEFORE... WAS IT AN OMEN? LIKE WHEN I SAW KATYA IN MY DREAM BEFORE SHE...?

THE NEXT NIGHT, DESPITE THE WITCH HUNTER, THE WITCHES WERE BACK ON MISSIONS. BEFORE THEY WENT UP, IRINA PASSED VERA A PARACHUTE.

WHAT ABOUT THE WEIGHT?

TRUST ME. I HAVE A FEELING WE WILL NEED THEM.

NOT LONG INTO THEIR FLIGHT, THEY WERE SPOTTED BY THE ENEMY.

UNNOTICED, HE STALKED THE WITCHES. THE GERMAN IMMEDIATELY ATTACKED HIS PREY, TAKING THEM BY SURPRISE.

BOZHE MOI! WHERE DID HE COME FROM?!

ALTHOUGH THEY WERE CAUGHT FLAT-FOOTED, IRINA AND VERA WERE DETERMINED TO PUT UP A FIGHT.

EAT SOVIET LEAD, NAZI RAT!

VERA'S BULLETS MET THEIR MARK.

GOTT IN HIMMEL!

HA-HA-HA!

BUT THE BULLETS DID LITTLE DAMAGE, AND ALREADY THE GERMAN WAS PREPARING HIS NEXT ATTACK.

IRINA DESPERATELY TRIED TO TURN THE PO-2 OUT OF THE PATH OF DANGER BUT IT WAS TOO LATE. BULLETS FROM THE NIGHT FIGHTER TORE INTO THE ENGINE.

HE'S GOT US! WE'LL HAVE TO BAIL OUT!

BAIL OUT?!

IT WAS ALL OVER SO FAST. ALTHOUGH SHE WAS ANGRY ABOUT THE OUTCOME OF THE DOGFIGHT, IRINA COULDN'T HELP BUT THINK OF HER DREAM AND FEEL RELIEVED.

I KNEW IT. I WAS RIGHT ABOUT THE PARACHUTES.

IRINA TOUCHED DOWN WITH LITTLE TROUBLE, BUT A PIT FORMED IN HER STOMACH AND SHE COULD INSTANTLY TELL SOMETHING WAS NOT RIGHT.

THAT'S WHEN SHE NOTICED THE SIGN.
NYET!
MINEN

VERA! WATCH OUT! IT'S A MINEFIELD!
WHAT?

IT WAS TOO LATE. AS SOON AS VERA LANDED IT WAS OVER, SHE WAS KILLED IMMEDIATELY BY THE MINE'S DETONATION.

AAAAH!

VERA? VERA!

NYET... NYET!

HER FRIEND WAS DEAD.

IRINA WAS SOON PICKED UP AND RETURNED TO THE BASE. SHE WAS GIVEN NO TIME TO GRIEVE. SHE FELT AWFUL AS SHE WAS GREETED BY TATYANA VOLKOVA.

PRIVET, COMRADE POPOVA, I'M YOUR NEW NAVIGATOR.

NEW? AND VERA BARELY IN THE GROUND.

POPOVA? YOU DON'T LOOK SO GOOD?

I'M... I'M FINE —

HELP! SOMEONE HELP!

FINALLY, IT WAS TOO MUCH. THE STRESS, THE FATIGUE AND ANXIETY HAD COME TO A HEAD, AND IRINA FELL TO THE GROUND.

AFTER COLLAPSING ON THE BASE, IRINA WAS SENT TO HOSPITAL TO REHABILITATE. EVERYONE COULD SEE SHE WAS A BAG OF NERVES, BARELY HOLDING IT TOGETHER.

IS THERE ANYTHING I CAN GET FOR YOU, IRINA?

COULD I HAVE A DRINK?

DA, I'LL GET YOU ONE NOW. YOU JUST REST UP.

AS THE NURSE LEFT THE ROOM, IRINA WAS ALERTED TO A SOUND AT THE WINDOW.

A BLACK CAT?

IRINA?
IRINA?

BY THE TIME THE NURSE HAD RETURNED, IRINA WAS NOWHERE TO BE FOUND.

BAREFOOT, SHE FOLLOWED, AND TOGETHER THEY WENT...

...INTO THE FOREST.

SEVERAL NIGHTS LATER, BACK AT THE 588TH CAMP, TATYANA WAS SURPRISED TO SEE IRINA WALKING OUT FROM THE DARKNESS OF THE NIGHT.

WHAT ARE YOU DOING HERE? I THOUGHT THEY SENT YOU TO THE HOSPITAL SO YOU COULD GET SOME REST?

DA, BUT I RAN AWAY. I COULDN'T RELAX WHILE I KNEW MY SISTERS CONTINUED TO FIGHT.

BUT WHAT ABOUT YOU? WILL YOU BE OKAY?

DON'T WORRY...

...I KNOW THAT I'LL BE ALL RIGHT FROM NOW ON. I'M A NIGHT WITCH AFTER ALL.

Cover: **JOAQUIN CHACOPINO FABRE**

Cover: **IAN KENNEDY**

Cover: **MARK HARRIS**

Cover: **IAN KENNEDY.** Commando #1289 'The Ghosts' (1979)

Cover: **TOM FOSTER.** Commando #5285 'Gaslight' (2019)

Cover: **NEIL ROBERTS.** Commando #5191 'Viking Phantom' (2019)

Cover: **GRAHAM MANLEY.** Commando #5585 'Frightful Tales' (2022)

Cover: **IAN KENNEDY.** Commando #1478 'Target — Crete!' (1981)

Cover: **NEIL ROBERTS.** Commando #5589 'Night of the Gorgons' (2022)

Cover: **NEIL ROBERTS.** Commando #5587 'Commandos vs Zombies 3' (2022)

Commando

FOR ACTION AND ADVENTURE

Since 1961, Commando Comics has electrified is readers as the longest-serving British war comic ever! Still printing today, and with over 5600 amazing issues, Commando has hunted through history to bring its audience thrilling tales of heroism, bravery, and comradery.

Suitable for ages 8-80+. These epic stories pack in 63 pages of classic black and white comic artwork set against global backdrops. With stories ranging from the Roman Era and other Ancient Empires, to Medieval and Viking combat, the World Wars, modern special forces, and even Future wars – there is something for all fans of history and comic art!

On land, at sea, and in the air, Commando has entertained readers for generations, as tales of friendship in the face of adversity take place in every corner of the world. What's more Commando is no stranger to Science Fiction and the Supernatural – as shown in this collection – with elements like ghouls and zombies, time travel and super albitites come into play as well!

Celebrated for its renowned artwork, with interiors and covers from British and international comic legends such as Ian Kennedy, Cam Kennedy, Gordon C Livingstone, Jordi Penalva and Jose Maria Jorge, the story illustrations are a crisp black and white, while Commando covers are always filled with explosive colour. Beautiful artwork combined with Commando's unaltered digest-size format make it the ideal comic for collectors.

Over sixty years later, Commando is proud to still be considered the Home of Heroes!

www.ingramcontent.com/pod-product-compliance
Lightning Source LLC
Chambersburg PA
CBHW081128020726
47505CB00010B/2278